Praise for

"Lively and entertain[...]...[...]r clever Edwardian tales with a gentle, loving touch. Ms. Browning's characters are imbued with class, charm, and wit, and the author has a strong grasp of time and place. The relationship is beautifully handled and a wee bit spicy."

—*Fresh Fiction*, Fresh Pick

"The nicely drawn characters and colorful backdrop allow readers to be drawn into a tender love story."

—*RT Book Reviews*

"Browning skillfully plays her characters off one another in a slow, charming manner, developing the relationship in a gentle fashion that doesn't disguise the simmering fire. The shifting morals and social rules of the time provide the perfect impetus for Alice's evolution and the story's resolution."

—*Publishers Weekly*

"Intriguing…a great read. The author does an incredible job at establishing a sense of time and place."

—*Night Owl Reviews*, Reviewer Top Pick

"There are characters you will love…the suspense is palpable and the last quarter of the book is shocking and clever all at once."

—*Romancing the Book*

Also by Sherri Browning

Thornbrook Park

An Affair Downstairs

The GREAT ESTATE

SHERRI BROWNING

sourcebooks
casablanca

Copyright © 2015 by Sherri Browning Erwin
Cover and internal design © 2015 by Sourcebooks, Inc.
Cover art by Paul Stinson

Sourcebooks and the colophon are registered trademarks of
Sourcebooks, Inc.

Published by Sourcebooks Casablanca, an imprint of Sourcebooks,
Inc.
P.O. Box 4410, Naperville, Illinois 60567-4410
(630) 961-3900
Fax: (630) 961-2168
www.sourcebooks.com

Printed and bound in Canada
MBP 10 9 8 7 6 5 4 3 2 1

For Margaret "Marg" Erwin. Peace.

One

SOPHIA, COUNTESS OF AVERFORD, ENDED UP EXACTLY as she'd always suspected she would: completely alone. She glanced up at her enormous portrait, hanging larger than life over the drawing room's marble fireplace, and sighed.

"We've done it now, darling girl," she said, looking into her own eyes, which were fixed in an imperious stare. "We've really done it."

What she had done was to give in to a kiss. No more than that. One passionate, toe-curling kiss. With a man who was not her husband. Didn't she deserve at least one kiss? Her husband hadn't kissed her in the longest time. When the Earl of Ralston had declared himself impossibly, irretrievably in love with her and had taken her in his arms, how was she to resist him?

Unfortunately, Gabriel, her husband, had walked in at the precise moment when she'd stopped pushing Ralston away and had pulled him to her instead. That one second of pull was all she'd needed, what she'd craved. In the moment, it didn't matter who'd taken command of her senses. But afterward?

Looking up over Ralston's shoulder and straight into the direct gaze of her husband in time to see his bright eyes cloud over with icy darkness, she knew that she had broken something in Gabriel, perhaps irreparably. He didn't storm, rail, or threaten murder, as she'd always suspected he would in such circumstances. He'd simply dropped his arms and walked away before she could regain her bearings and run after him.

They'd never spoken of it. They barely spoke at all. Her marriage had fallen into a shambles, and after months of few words and mounting hostility between them, Gabriel had packed his things and had joined his mother in Italy, leaving Sophia alone at Thornbrook Park. To add insult to injury, he hadn't entrusted her with command of his beloved estate.

He probably didn't believe her capable of organizing much beyond her own closet, and that only with the assistance of her reliable lady's maid. Gabriel's land agent, Cornelius Kenner, reported to Gabriel by letter once a week and then executed all of Gabriel's orders as they came in by telegraph. Or so Gabriel had been led to believe.

In her husband's absence, Sophia had taken charge. Why shouldn't she? Thornbrook Park was her home too, and Cornelius Kenner was dreadfully not up to the task. Sophia would have sacked him if not for fear that news would get back to Gabriel and he'd return on the next boat to give her hell. She wanted her husband back, but not until he was ready to return.

Not until he was so desperate to see her that he would beg her forgiveness for running off and promise her the moon and stars for want of her affection.

Until then, she welcomed the challenge of keeping the estate in the best possible condition, perhaps even improving it where she could. For all intents and purposes, every servant needed to believe that Kenner was managing the estate, with Sophia only offering an opinion from time to time. Kenner was none too eager to publicly acknowledge his own incompetence and thus agreeable to Sophia's plan. His salary remained the same, and he maintained his successful image.

A year later, the lawyers, the butler, the footmen and maids, even Mrs. Hoyle, Kenner's cousin by blood, remained convinced of the ruse. Only once Gabriel returned would Sophia admit the truth. She would show her husband, and everyone, that she was a woman of sense and substance, a woman who would not be denied her heart's desire.

After a year on her own, she knew beyond any doubt that her heart's desire was to win back her husband's love, or at least to earn his respect. Respect should be guaranteed, considering the estate was thriving after a year in her capable hands. In fact, Thornbrook Park had been running at an increased profit, thanks in part to Mr. Wesley Grant, a brilliant strategist she'd lured away from Mrs. Alva Belmont, a visiting American.

Mr. Grant had come along filled with ideas of how to more effectively manage and find new economic opportunities for Thornbrook Park. Economic opportunities? Such a vulgar concept, but one she easily forgave from an American. She'd politely listened to Grant's ideas over tea, and she'd agreed to give him a chance after consulting her brother-in-law, Logan Winthrop, for his opinion.

Before Mr. Kenner, Winthrop had been their most capable agent until he married Alice and swept her off to Stratton Place and then to India, the Orient, Africa… Sophia lost track of where her sister was at any given moment. The Winthrops seemed to have plans to cover the whole world before coming home again.

Winthrop had suggested she hire Grant and send Kenner on his way. The Winthrops had gone off to India before confirming whether Sophia had taken the chance. Grant's official position was as Sophia's personal secretary, and Kenner's was estate agent, but each performed the other's job and neither seemed to mind it. Gabriel had raised questions when Mr. Kenner wrote to him regarding Mr. Grant's salary, but the earl had agreed to it in the end.

"Give her what she wants," he had written, full stop, leaving Sophia to guess at his mood or his intentions when he wrote it. She imagined him railing to his mother about all of his wife's supposed failings.

"Lord knows, she will take it without any regard to my feelings on the matter…" Or "She hasn't the sense to know she's overpaying…" Or worse, "What do I care what that woman does now? She's nothing to me…"

For all Sophia knew, her husband had consulted with his solicitor to discuss the possibility of divorce. She sat at the brink of despair, mulling over the possibility, until her aunt Agatha swept into the room as if to remind Sophia that she would never be completely alone, should everyone else abandon her.

"Dear girl, light some lamps! Nothing good can come of sitting alone in the dark." Agatha paused a moment as if to reconsider. "Not entirely true, of course. I've had some of my best moments alone in the dark, but we're very different, aren't we? The dark doesn't suit you, my dear."

"Has it grown dark? Indeed you're right. I hadn't noticed." Sophia remained as limp as a discarded doll in her chair.

Agatha closed the distance between them, switching on lights as she approached. Even before Sophia's eyes could adjust to the light, she had a clear image of Agatha in her fire-orange and aubergine ensemble. Her aunt settled on the sofa beside Sophia.

"I've had a letter from your mother."

It wasn't unusual for the sisters to be in communication, but something in her aunt's tone told Sophia that unexpected information was to follow. She straightened up a bit. "Yes? And how is everyone at Delaney Square?"

"They're all well. Even your father." Agatha didn't hide her disappointment with that bit of news. She'd never gotten on with Sophia's father. Sophia had done her best to keep them apart at Alice's wedding to avoid any unpleasantness. "It seems that she wrote with news that concerns you. She always was such a gossip, you know."

Sophia waved her hand dismissively. "I know. Her intricate web of tittering busybodies could rival the king's own network of spies."

Brow furrowed, Agatha placed a hand on Sophia's knee. "Gabriel's back."

Sophia looked left and right. Agatha considered herself in communication with the spirit world and liked to read fortunes, but she probably didn't mean her comment in the literal sense. Sophia assumed she meant that Gabriel's essence was in the air, or some such nonsense. "Where?"

"In London, dear."

"At Averford House?" Sophia tried to contain her surprise. She hated London. Their house in town stood empty most of the time, unless Gabriel went to London to tend to parliamentary affairs. "In London? Now?"

Agatha nodded. "Lady Levesque told your mother that he has been there this past month. A fortnight at least. I'm not certain exactly when he arrived."

"But he's there. And he didn't see fit to inform me that he'd returned to England?" Her heart dropped like a lead ball to the pit of her stomach. She rose and began to pace, no longer bothering to hide her distress at the news. "Not a word to me. Not a word to Mr. Kenner? Or do you think he knows? Kenner knows. And who else? Have they been instructed not to tell me? Or do they pity me too much to say a word?"

Agatha stood and came to her side. "Don't become agitated. I don't think anyone knows. Of course, the people in London know. Or so it seems. He has been carrying on as usual."

"As usual?" Sophia cocked a brow. Only now did it occur to her to ask what her husband did in London when she did not go with him. "Carrying on?"

Dread, cold as ice, snaked up her spine.

Agatha shrugged. "Attending dinners. Musicales. Perhaps the theater? He's a respected man, an earl. There are always invitations and the responsibility for a man to attend such things."

"Of course." Sophia gripped the back of a Chippendale chair. "Responsibilities. He must have come back for a vote. Parliament. How long could he stay away, after all? A man in his position."

"Exactly." Agatha clapped her hands. "That sort of thing. How long could he avoid such business? There's talk of reform…"

"What reform?"

"There's always reform, dear. The Trade Boards Act, the Labour Exchanges Act…"

Sophia narrowed her eyes. "You follow politics, Aunt Agatha?"

Agatha tilted her head. "As one does. It's important to keep up with current affairs, don't you think?"

"As one does." Suddenly, Sophia felt more inadequate than usual. She'd never paid attention to such things. It simply wasn't ladylike to follow politics, as Mother always said. But Mother had been wrong about so many things, and they weren't living under Queen Victoria's rule any longer. It was a brandnew day.

"Lord Osborne probably urged him to return for one cause or another." Agatha shrugged. "An important vote on the line or something of the sort. Men do get so caught up in it all. There probably wasn't enough time to send word."

"Or even telephone? It wouldn't take more than

instructing Sutton to telephone Finch and have Finch let me know. Or a telegram, if he couldn't be bothered with more." The butlers of their London and Yorkshire houses remained in communication as needed. As much as Finch had been hesitant to use the telephone, he had finally come around.

Agatha closed her eyes and fluttered her fingers in the air. "The spirits are active. I think we can trust that Lord Averford will be finding his way home soon."

"How do you know? Do the spirits share such information?" Sophia cast another glance around the room. "Are they here now? Ghosts?"

"Just Miss Puss." Agatha gestured across the room. "She's sitting in Lord Averford's favorite chair, a sure sign she is anticipating his return."

"Just Miss Puss," Sophia echoed. Miss Puss was Agatha's most devoted companion, a ghost cat that she had brought with her when she moved from the Dower House to a suite in Thornbrook Park. In fact, Sophia had resorted to sending a footman over to "catch" the elusive Miss Puss in a hatbox when Agatha threatened not to leave the Dower House without her.

Fortunately, Agatha believed Miss Puss had taken a liking to Bill, the footman, and showed up to follow him without need of the box. They'd all come to accept the cat as real, whether or not she lived only in Agatha's imagination. No one but Agatha had ever seen Miss Puss.

"I wish I had more of a sign," Sophia said. "Miss Puss could simply be missing Gabriel."

Agatha shrugged. "Perhaps it's time to take matters into your own hands, my dear. Write to him. Or telephone."

"You're right, Aunt. Of course." She filled with sudden inspiration. "Why didn't I think of it right away?"

"Think of what? Telephoning or writing?"

Sophia rang for Mr. Kenner. "Nothing of the sort. I don't want Gabriel to have any warning of my arrival."

"But you don't mean to—" Agatha was interrupted by the appearance of Mr. Kenner.

The man hesitated in the doorway as he awaited orders, pushing his spectacles up on his nose in a manner that added gravitas, if not age, to his thin frame. He still parted his fair hair in the middle, like a schoolboy, and slicked it back at the sides.

"Yes, Lady Averford?"

"Kenner, make the necessary preparations. I'm going to London."

"London?" Kenner and Agatha echoed at once. "But you hate London."

She nodded. "Yes, I know. Apparently everyone knows." Kenner must have heard it from the other servants, the gossips. She didn't remember ever sharing the information with him directly. "But if that's where Gabriel intends to stay, then I mean to join him there. Our estrangement has gone on long enough."

Or at least she'd let him stay away long enough. It was time to remind him what he was missing before he concluded he could very well get on without her. She only hoped it wasn't too late.

The Earl of Averford's boots slammed the cobble-
stones with force, a somewhat jarring sensation considering the worn state of his soles. New boots, fine
Italian leather. He should have known not to relent
to wearing such frippery, but for once he'd listened
to his mother.

"A fine man needs fine clothes," she'd said.
"Delicately spun silks. The softest kidskin. Textures
sensual to the touch. You want to impress Sophia with
how much you've changed."

A man could only change so much. He was a man
of sport, not style. Good English boots could stand up
to months of traipsing through wilderness. The fop-
pish Italian riders had given out after a mere fortnight
of pacing London's streets.

In truth, he had done an extraordinary amount of
pacing since leaving Thornbrook Park. He'd worn
a crevice in the stone floors of his mother's Italian
palazzo. In London, he preferred to channel his pent-up
frustrations into walking the streets instead of treading
his Aubusson carpets threadbare. He had determined
that he wouldn't return to Sophia until he'd become
a better man, a romantic man, someone who knew
about paintings, music, literature, and the art of love.

He aimed to show her that he cared about the very
things that impressed her most, the finer things, and
that she needn't look any further for a skilled lover
than in their own boudoir. It had taken him years to
understand that he had gone about being a husband all
wrong. Only catching her in the arms of another man
seemed to have wakened him to the reality that he'd
failed her. Miserably.

Once he'd gotten over his anger, of course. His first reaction had been one of murderous rage, but one glance at his former estate manager, who had stumbled on the scene at the same moment, calmed him. Winthrop, a man shadowed by an act of rage for half his life, had learned to face any challenge with level-headed shrewdness. In that instant, Gabriel became determined to follow Winthrop's stoic example.

If Gabriel's wife wanted to kiss another man, who was he to stop her? Killing her lover wouldn't win her affection back. Besides, Sophia craved drama the way some yearned for a tincture of opium. She might have arranged the whole performance specifically to get a reaction out of him. For the entire holiday season, she had been out of sorts.

"Who could blame the poor woman, out of her mind with fear for her sister?" His mother had defended Sophia.

Sophia's sister had been thrown from a horse and was recuperating from serious injuries at Thornbrook Park. That accounted for the presence of Lord Ralston, a supposed admirer of Alice's. Gabriel was not surprised that the bounder had been using Alice as an excuse to stick close to the real object of his affection, Sophia.

Admittedly, Gabriel had practically ignored Sophia in her time of need and had allowed the situation to escalate by giving Ralston every opportunity to turn Sophia's heightened emotional state to his advantage and attempt a seduction. Gabriel had realized the man's intentions too late and then failed to act on his suspicions in time. It shouldn't have come as a surprise to find the man attempting to woo his wife and yet…Gabriel had been flabbergasted at the sight of them.

Nearly from the start, he'd blamed no one but himself, but he'd been too ashamed to address the subject with Sophia. He wasn't accustomed to failure, particularly at such a personal level. Communication between them had been difficult at best since the loss of their infant son, neither of them knowing quite what to say to the other.

"These things just happen sometimes," the doctor had explained. "You put a perfectly healthy-looking newborn to bed, and he simply never wakes up."

Their little Edward and all of their hopes and dreams had been buried in the ground. Gabriel had been at a complete loss about how to comfort his wife when his own grief had pierced like a flame-hot dagger through his raw heart. And now, like then, Gabriel had found he was at a loss for words.

Gabriel's brother, Marcus, had been born with their father's silver tongue. Gabriel had learned to make use of more physical skills to make a point, but he'd clearly become a better fighter than a lover. In that way, he hoped he had changed. He aimed to show Sophia what he'd learned in Italy from paying close attention to the masters of love: poets, musicians, philosophers, and artists. The only way to make amends was to seduce her, body and soul.

"What's on your mind, Averford? You're dreadfully quiet." His companion, Lord Wilkerson, struck the ground pointedly with his walking stick as they made their way back to a parliamentary session from the pub. "But then, you've never been one for idle chatter."

Seducing his own wife? Hardly a confession to make to one's peer. "Boots. I'm thinking of my boots, Wilkerson. Damned uncomfortable."

"Boots are passé, Averford, but then you would hardly know that, staying away from London for so long. What you need is a good pair of shoes with bulldog toes, maybe some spats." Wilkerson stopped walking and pulled his trouser leg up an inch to display his footwear, black shoes that bulged up a little at the rounded toe.

Gabriel laughed. "You think to make me into a fop like you, Wilkie?"

"Not a fop." Wilkerson colored at the suggestion, his thin mustache looking more white than silver in contrast with his brightened cheeks. "A man of style."

"Have you met my mother, Wilkerson? It occurs to me that the two of you would make quite a pair."

"Your mother?" He stroked his pointed chin. "Can't say that I've had the pleasure. In Italy, isn't she?"

Gabriel shook his head. "Paris. She's ordering a new wardrobe."

"Yes, ladies and their finery. I do appreciate a well-attired woman."

"To each his own. I prefer them without a stitch." Gabriel flashed a roguish grin. The idea of making love to Sophia had become a constant distraction. He'd meant to stay in London for a few weeks, enough time to make up for neglecting his parliamentary responsibilities, but nothing mattered more to him than making up with his own wife. "If you'll excuse me, I think I'll look into new shoes. Bullfrog toe, you say?"

"Bulldog, man. Bull. Dog. You'll thank me. But don't run off now! We're almost there. We've got to vote."

"The vote will pass without me, Wilkie. You make a very persuasive argument on the rights of the poor and the good of all men, and so on. I simply can't wait another minute for those shoes. Good day." Gabriel tipped his hat and ran off before Wilkerson could make another argument to stop him.

If he hurried back to Averford House and urged Sutton to pack only the most necessary things, he could be on the train back to Thornbrook Park in no time.

Two

SOPHIA HAD NO EARTHLY IDEA WHAT SHE WOULD SAY to her husband when she saw him again after nearly a year apart. Perhaps she would carry on as if nothing had happened, simply pick up where they'd left off before everything had gone so wrong between them. By now, what else was there to say?

"Oh, sorry I kissed Lord Ralston, by the way. How was Italy?"

She took a deep breath as the cab pulled up in front of Averford House. To mask her trepidation at surprising her husband, she put on the imperious face she wore when dealing with the servants and smiled coolly at the driver as he opened the door for her to step out.

"Thank you. A footman will see to compensating you when he comes to retrieve my luggage."

Before the driver could protest, she walked by him, up the steps to the door, and entered. No one was there to greet her, as expected since she hadn't called ahead. She proceeded to the parlor and rang for Sutton.

"My lady." His cheeks reddened in surprise as he rounded the corner. "I—we weren't expecting you."

Finch, their Yorkshire butler, had the good sense to appear unruffled at all times. Sutton occasionally slipped and revealed himself to be…human, she supposed. The man was only human. Why would she expect otherwise? Times were changing, as her friend Eve never failed to remind her. Perhaps it was time Sophia softened her expectations. A little. But allowing the servants to be human meant that she might slip and expose herself as human too. She wasn't sure she wanted to make herself that vulnerable.

"Of course not." She loosened her lace gloves one finger at a time and pulled them off. "I came on a whim. I'm sorry if I've startled you. I hope it won't be much trouble to make my room ready, considering Lord Averford is already in house."

It was the first time she'd ever apologized to a servant that she could recall, and she supposed that she could do it again. The foundation hadn't rocked beneath her feet, and Sutton remained standing before her awaiting further instruction. Surely Gabriel might see it as a sign that she was making an effort.

"Lord Averford? Oh. Yes, well…"

"Take my coat, Sutton." She shrugged out of it and held it aloft. "And do go out with the footman to get my luggage. I haven't a bob to tip the driver. That's what you do when you take a taxi, yes? Tip the driver?"

Sutton nodded and took her coat to hang. "I'll take care of everything, Lady Averford. Please make yourself at home. I'll return in a moment."

With that, the man ran off to see to the business at

hand. Sophia walked around, taking in the ambience of their house in town. It was all as she remembered, though she hadn't seen it in quite some time. The enormous flower arrangement on the round marble table in the hall was practically the only feminine touch in a predominantly male space, adding a hint of brightness to an otherwise dark environment.

The entry hall's walls were paneled in mahogany, giving way to forest-green watered silk in the parlor and burgundy in the drawing room, where two large wingback chairs framed the austere green marble fireplace. No wonder Gabriel's brother had fallen into such a lull here before his return to Thornbrook Park. The place could use some brightening up. If she stayed in town long enough, she fancied she might discover a new artist to paint some sunny landscapes.

"Forgive me, my lady." Sutton returned apologetic moments later. "I've given half the staff or more the day off, not realizing we would be in need of them now that the master has gone."

"Gone?" In astonishment, Sophia dropped a hand from the necklace she'd been twisting out of habit. "What do you mean, gone?"

Sutton shrugged. "He returned to Thornbrook Park on the morning train. I thought you knew. Perhaps he meant to surprise you?"

"Exactly what I'm doing here, Sutton, attempting to surprise him. Aren't we a pair?" She added a brittle laugh when she really wanted to cry. She'd come all the way to London for nothing.

"I'll call one of the maids to get you settled. No need to go rushing back now. It's late. Cook's preparing a simple meal of creamed chicken, but I'll have her get started on something more elaborate."

"No need." Sophia blinked back her tears and stiffened her spine. "Simple creamed chicken sounds lovely, as long as there are peas. I do like peas in my creamed chicken."

Sutton's mouth gaped for a brief second before he tightened his lips into a severe line. Clearly, he'd expected her to make more demands. "I believe there are peas and potatoes, Lady Averford. But I'll check to make sure."

"Very good, Sutton. Send the maid up to my room to unpack my things and bring me the newspaper. I believe I'll catch up on politics." She sat in one of the wingback chairs and smoothed her hands over the fabric on the arms, a forest-green velvet wearing thin. She would have the chairs reupholstered.

"Politics?" He shook his head as if sorry to have asked. "Of course. I'll bring it right away. And some tea?"

"Tea would be just the thing."

With a nod, he left her. She closed her eyes, tipped her head back, and sighed. One night in London wouldn't be the death of her. She would make a list of all the things that needed updating and leave it with Sutton upon her departure in the morning. What would Gabriel think, she wondered, when he got to Thornbrook Park to find that she had gone to London? Considering all the times he'd tried and failed to tempt her to travel with him, he might think she was meeting a lover. Oh dear. She sat up, alarmed. And what if he consulted Mr. Kenner for a report on the management of Thornbrook Park?

She eased back into the cushion. If she had learned anything in the past year, it was that there was no point in worrying when she couldn't control the outcome. Gabriel would believe what he wanted, and he would find out the truth about Kenner and Grant soon enough, most likely before she got back to control the damage.

Before the butler could return to her, the doorbell rang. A minute later, Sutton announced the Earl of Wilkerson. She rose to greet him.

"You've returned to us." He delivered a brief, dry kiss to the back of her hand, his intimacy startling her. She didn't think he could possibly remember her well from their brief meeting some five or eight years ago. She barely remembered him except from Gabriel's occasional stories. "So good to see you, and in the prime of health."

The prime of health? Did he think her ill? Perhaps Gabriel had made excuses for her absence. "I am well, Lord Wilkerson. What brings you to Averford House?"

"I came to call on your son, but I seem to have missed him. No matter. I find I'm left to better, or at least lovelier, company, Lady Averford." He arched a brow and grinned. Was he flirting with her? Had the story of her downfall reached so widely that he thought he might take liberties with his friend's wife? Ah, but he said that he'd come to call on her son...

"My son, Lord Wilkerson? I'm afraid you're mistaken. I have no son." No son. Even now, she felt a hollow ache to speak it aloud.

He stroked his thin, silver mustache with a gloved hand. "I can see why you might feel that way, with him running off to Yorkshire instead of staying to greet you properly. Come." He cradled her elbow and steered her toward the sofa in the opposite corner of the room. "Let's have a seat and see if I can comfort you with conversation."

She pulled her arm away. "Forgive me for being rude, sir, but I've only just arrived after a journey. I must ask you to leave. I'll have my husband inform you when he means to return to Averford House."

"Your husband? But I thought you'd never remarried after his passing."

"Lord Wilkerson!" Dear God, for some reason the man took her to be her mother-in-law. "If you wear spectacles, this might be a good time to put them on."

She prayed he wore spectacles, else she would have to accept that she looked as old as a woman more than twice her age.

"I do. How did you know?" He fiddled in his coat pocket, pulled them out, put them on, and wrinkled up his nose as his eyes adjusted. "Lady Averford. I must apologize. I believed you were the Dowager Countess come from Paris."

"She's in Italy." Where Sophia prayed the woman would stay.

"If you say so. I'm not one to correct you after the terrible mistake I've just made. Please do forgive me, Lady Averford. Indeed, I can hardly see a thing without my spectacles. Your husband informed me that his mother might be receptive to, ah, to attention, I suppose, and I certainly didn't mean to offend you."

Gabriel trying to make a match, after all the lectures she'd endured from him when she'd tried to do the same? She couldn't begin to imagine. "No offense taken, Lord Wilkerson. I am truly sorry that you missed Lord Averford. I'll be joining him shortly at Thornbrook Park, and I will be certain to share your regards."

"Yes, do. And tell him to hurry back. I'm not sure the vote will pass without him. He knows which one I mean."

"Are you sure?"

"The Labour Exchanges Act, of course. We're eager to make it easier for the unemployed to find work."

"You are? He is?" Gabriel taking a keen interest in the plight of his fellow man? She had no idea he was involved with such important and benevolent legislation. "Yes, well, I will let him know that he's needed."

At Thornbrook Park. In her bed. She'd never missed him as acutely as she had in turning up at Averford House to find him gone. How she wanted him here with her! She rang for Sutton and he appeared not a moment later.

"Please show Lord Wilkerson out, Mr. Sutton. Thank you for calling, Lord Wilkerson." She couldn't manage to add the simplest pleasantry in parting. Mistaking her for her mother-in-law? Unforgiveable, really.

As soon as she'd settled with the newspaper and her tea following Lord Wilkerson's departure, she heard the doorbell peal again.

"Who could it be now?" she said aloud to no one.

The answer followed Sutton in before any formal announcement could be made.

"Lord Markham." She stood, eager to greet her

friend. The Markhams had been part of their social circle at Thornbrook Park until Lord Markham married a silly young woman who insisted he sell their Yorkshire estate and relocate. Sophia couldn't complain, since they'd sold the estate to Gabriel's brother and her dearest friend, Eve, but she did miss Lord Markham, if not his ridiculous wife. "How lovely to see you. Come in."

She meant every word. She was quite at home with her friend Markham, a good man who would never mistake her for the Dowager Countess.

"My dear Lady Averford! I never expected to see you here. I came around to see if your husband wanted to go for supper at the pub."

"Supper at the pub, Lord Markham? Is that something the pair of you do here in London? How does Lady Markham feel about that?" She imagined the shrewish woman flying into a temper. *A pub? Leaving me here at home alone?*

"Sometimes we go to the pub. He's lonely here without you."

Did he say so to Lord Markham? A tingle skittered along her nerves. Gabriel really missed her? "London is a lonely place, if you ask me. So many people, but not so many to care about, excepting present company of course."

"Kind of you to say." He smiled without mirth. He'd always had such a twinkle in his silver-gray eyes, but the twinkle was absent at the moment. He looked rather worn down. She would ring Sutton to bring him some tea.

"More than words, Lord Markham. We've known

each other far too long for cool politeness. Please call me Sophia. It's about time, don't you think?"

"Sophia, yes." He brightened. "You must call me Charles then, of course. And Lady Markham couldn't have a care on the subject of my dining at the pub one way or another. I'm sorry to say that we've divorced."

"Divorced?" Sophia could hardly contain her gasp. How had such news failed to reach her at Thornbrook Park? A divorce! Shocking. All the more distressing when it concerned a dear old friend. Still, she couldn't help feeling that he was better off, as long as his fortune remained mostly intact.

"Charles." She placed a hand on his arm. "I'm so sorry. What a terrible time for you."

"It has been almost a year. She ran off with her vocal coach. The man said he could make her a star on the stage, and I foolishly agreed to pay for her lessons. I've heard whispers that she has ended up on a stage, all right, but not at an establishment that anyone of quality would frequent, if you understand my meaning."

"Oh dear, I think I might. Forget the pub, Lord— Charles. Dine here with me. Simple fare, but good company. We're having creamed chicken with peas and potatoes."

"Creamed chicken? Not your usual spread, Sophia." She was known for her elaborate dinner parties. "But it does sound tempting. I would love to stay."

"Then it's settled. I'll ring for Sutton to set an extra plate at the table. And in the meantime, would you like some tea?"

⤞⤝

Thornbrook Park. A warm wave of pride filled Gabriel at the sight as Dale drove them up the winding way. The chimneys appeared first over the crest of the hill, followed by the slate roof, and finally the rose stone facade. How could he have stayed away so long?

Sophia wouldn't be expecting him. He planned to surprise her, perhaps persuade Finch not to even announce his return. He would simply appear at the dinner hour, dressed to the nines, and act as if he had been there the entire time. *Darling, I believe the quail is cooked perfectly, but not quite the same as when I shoot it myself…* No, that wouldn't do. She hated it when he left her alone to go off hunting.

He'd always known that, but he couldn't seem to give it up. Old habits. In truth, he couldn't wait to get his boots on, the good English ones he'd left behind, take up his rifle, and stomp off into the woods. His woods. Alas, there would be no more hunting. At least not as frequently, and certainly not right away. Not until he knew that he wouldn't upset Sophia further. Not until she forgave him.

Perhaps he could suggest other activities they could do together. His brow shot up. He knew just what activity he had in mind, but they would have to work up to that. Slowly. He meant to court her properly, one step at a time.

"Now, Dale, I don't want a fuss," he said. "It's good to be home but no need for a celebration. I mean to slip in quietly."

"Mr. Finch wouldn't share the news, my lord. I was at his side when he took your call and promised not to tell a soul except me, not even Mrs. Mallows. She makes enough to feed an army even though it's usually just the countess and Mr. Grant dining formally."

"Mr. Grant?" Gabriel felt his heart skip a beat. He recalled Kenner writing him about this man Grant's salary, an exorbitant sum for a personal secretary, but he didn't want to question Sophia's motives at the time. He only wanted her to be happy. But who was this Grant fellow? Perhaps he should have investigated more thoroughly. "The secretary, Grant, joins her for dinner? Is he a good fellow?"

Sophia allowing one of the servants, even one of the upper echelon, to dine with her? It wasn't like her. She liked to keep everyone in the proper place, and her place was always much above everyone else's. Always. She enjoyed the distinction of being a countess.

Dale shrugged. "I haven't spoken with him at length. He seems like a decent sort, once you get past the brash American tones."

"Right. He was previously employed by the Belmonts, I believe. And he dines with Lady Averford every evening?" Unbelievable.

"Almost every evening." Dale nodded as he turned the car toward the front of the house. "As far as I know. Not last night though, of course."

"Take us around the back, Dale. I don't want a lot of fuss, as I said. Perhaps I can just sneak in without anyone knowing and surprise Lady Averford at dinner. Why not last night?"

"You didn't know?" Dale sounded surprised. "Oh, I'm sorry, Lord Averford. The countess was preparing for her journey. She went to London on the morning train."

"London?" What could possibly have drawn her to the place? Had she heard that he was in town?

He'd tried to keep a low profile, going out as little as possible. Though Wilkie had dragged him along to that one reception, insisting they had to put in an appearance to drum up more votes for the Labour Exchanges Act. He hadn't stayed long, a few minutes at best. Long enough for word to get out, apparently. Sophia had probably heard it from her mother. He should never underestimate the woman's reach. Sophia's mother might not get out much anymore, but she always seemed to know everything going on in London.

"To see you, perhaps," Dale said. "I thought you'd had words before you left, or I would have said something."

"Of course. Our paths must have crossed."

"At any rate, welcome home, sir."

"Thank you, Dale." Gabriel let himself out of the car, not waiting for the chauffeur to come around for the door.

He took his time heading in, reacquainting himself with the grounds as he ambled. The gardens, the garden house, the fields and orchards beyond, and the air! He breathed it deeply, a restorative balm to his soul. The fresh, clean air of Thornbrook Park. There was nothing quite like it. Not even in Arezzo, Siena, or Florence. Most especially not in Florence. All too well, he remembered the stench of unwashed bodies crowded into the Baptistry of St. John. He removed his hat and waved it around, stirring the air so he could get another gulp.

He planned to go straight to the kitchen, where he would casually ask Mrs. Mallows for a glass of lemonade. It was a warm day and there should be an abundance of lemons from the trees his mother had sent some time ago. Mrs. Mallows would startle at the sight of him, perhaps even call out for Mrs. Hoyle, Mr. Finch, and any other of the servants within earshot. How happy he would be to greet them all!

But no Sophia, the one he wanted most to see, his lovely wife. Beyond lovely. He'd been all over Europe and back, and he had yet to meet a woman who could outshine his own wife. Her staggering beauty had been the first thing he'd noticed about her, so much that he'd forgotten to breathe in her presence more than once. The stunning combination of her raven hair, ivory skin, and cornflower-blue eyes made her nearly impossible to miss and, once glimpsed, absolutely incapable of being forgotten. No wonder Lord Ralston had tried to win her over. What man could resist?

The memory of their wedding night remained his most extraordinary memory to date, the best day of his life barring the day their son was born, which was also the most tragic considering... But that was best left unexplored for now. The pain of losing Edward had cast him into a downward spiral that had lasted for half a year, if not more, and he did not care to relive it.

The memory of his wedding night, however, brought him great joy and he became lost in the recollection of it all too often. Sophia's gasp when he peeled her gown from her delicate, white shoulders. His first sight of her breasts, slight but symmetrical, enough to fill his hand, and tipped with rosy nipples that hardened at his touch. The way her abdomen tensed and shook when he parted her tender thighs and blew a steady stream of air on her navel, then lower.

She'd sobbed in his arms that first time, and he'd been alarmed until she'd explained that she always cried when she was so supremely happy. Happier than she had ever been. The pain was hardly anything, she'd said, and hadn't lasted as long as she'd feared when she first glimpsed him. He wasn't a small man, and he felt a secret thrill that he'd managed to intimidate her with the sight of him, and an even greater satisfaction when he learned he'd pleased her more than hurt her. Aglow with youthful pride, he'd congratulated himself on his apparently tremendous skill in his wife's bed. She'd quaked! She'd trembled! She'd cried! Clearly, he was a god.

But it hadn't happened again, not with such a strong reaction, and he began to doubt his prowess. She'd been a virgin, untried, unsure what to expect, and he had impressed her. But after that? He'd tried everything he could think of to bring her to the brink of bliss, and none of it seemed to occasion more than a contented sigh. A tolerant sigh most often, if he were being honest.

Once, when experimenting with a new position, turning her around to take her from behind, she'd squealed and slapped him, letting him know that he'd gone beyond his bounds. Finally, when the idea of going to her bedroom began to fill him with more dread than anticipation, he'd become desperate enough to consider going to his brother for advice. His brother had been quite a favorite with the ladies before he'd gone off to war.

But by the time Gabriel got his courage up to ask, his brother had been shipped off. Fortunately, Sophia had hinted that the maid was letting out all her gowns, and it had dawned on him what such news meant only moments later.

"Are you?" he'd asked.

"Yes!" she'd said, and she began to cry in the same way she had on their first night together, a sure sign that she was beyond delighted too.

And then after Edward's unexpected death, there'd been next to nothing between them ever again. They shared moments of intimacy, true, but nothing more than glances, smiles, or a touch of the hand. She'd become afraid to let him do more than barely touch her, too frightened of becoming pregnant again and losing another baby.

As soon as he'd caught her in Ralston's arms, he knew that he should have fought harder to convince her to try again. He'd thought she'd closed herself off from feeling any kind of deep emotion, but clearly he'd been wrong. She yearned for love as much as he did, perhaps more. There was no reason they couldn't find their way back to each other now after all his time and care in Italy learning how to be more responsive to her needs. No reason at all.

Breathing the Yorkshire air cleared his mind so that he could see a way forward at last. He knew what he had to do next.

Three

LISTENING TO LORD MARKHAM'S PROBLEMS HAD encouraged Sophia to feel better about her own. She needed to speak with Gabriel. Tomorrow, she would head straight back to Thornbrook Park. But for tonight, she would try to be a proper hostess and take Lord Markham's mind off his troubles.

He was highly entertained when she told him that Lord Wilkerson had mistaken her for Gabriel's mother.

"Dodgy old fool." Markham shook his head and reached for the bottle to pour them more wine, but the footman beat him to the task after a pointed look from Sutton as if to remind him. "He can't see a thing without his spectacles. Once, months ago, he tried to change from spectacles to a monocle. With only one bad eye accommodated, he went all wonky and fell right off the curb on the short stroll from Parliament to the pub. No matter. It led him to his next favorite affectation, the walking stick."

"Oh dear. We don't see many of those in Yorkshire."

"How I miss home!"

"You can always return. You're welcome at

Thornbrook Park, and I'm certain the Thornes would allow you to have a look around your old house."

Their conversation was interrupted by another ringing of the doorbell. Sutton left his post and, a moment later, reappeared with Marcus and Eve Thorne. "Oh, look who's here."

"Stay seated, please," Marcus urged.

"Yes, don't get up on our account," Eve agreed. "We'll join you."

Sutton went off, probably to get more place settings, as Marcus and Eve took their seats. "Lord Markham, a pleasure to find you here. We haven't seen you in some time," Marcus said. "How are you?"

"Not as well as could be hoped. I've been keeping to myself mostly, avoiding the gossips."

"Oh dear, the divorce." Eve, seated next to him, reached out and patted his hand. "I'm so sorry. I couldn't believe the news. It must have come as such a shock."

"I can't say that you're not indirectly to blame in some small part, Mrs. Thorne. Forgive me for causing any offense."

"Me to blame?" Eve's pale blue eyes widened in shock. "What could I have done?"

Marcus sat on the edge of his seat, ready to argue in his wife's defense. Sophia suddenly envied her friend a husband who would stand up for her. There was a time when Gabriel would have done the same, but that time had passed.

"Romantic novels!" Markham threw his hands up in exasperation. "She couldn't get enough of them. Yours and many others. Reading about so many love affairs must have fueled her desire to have one of her own."

Sophia bit her lip, nervous about her friend's reaction. Eve had been writing novels for years to great acclaim and success, but apparently not to Lord Markham's liking.

Eve tipped her head back and laughed. "My dear Lord Markham, you can't really suppose reading romantic novels inspired your wife's actions! Some men like murder mysteries, but I doubt reading them makes those men any more inclined to kill."

"I'm sorry." He shrugged resignedly. "I suppose you're right."

"Do you miss her?" Eve asked. "When you really think about it, didn't you always believe that you were unsuited?"

Markham paused to think a moment before continuing. "I miss companionship. But I suppose you're right. Olivia and I were not of the same mind on many things."

"You see? It was your incompatibility and not Olivia's reading habits that drove a wedge between you. Perhaps you should start reading romantic novels, Lord Markham. I have a new one coming out in a few months, which is what brought us to London without the children. We're staying for a few more days."

"A few days?" Sophia was sorry to hear it. "I was hoping you would accompany me back to Thornbrook Park. Gabriel has returned."

"Yes, I wondered what brought you all the way to London, Sophia." Eve sat back to allow Sutton to serve her. "Do regale us with the story as we eat."

With a sigh, Sophia began to recount how she'd heard about Gabriel's homecoming. It didn't bother her that Lord Markham was a guest at the table. He'd been open with her about his own problems, and she felt closer to him for it. She would spare no details.

⁂

Gabriel closed the ledger, tented his fingers, and faced Mr. Kenner across his desk. Kenner slumped in the chair, avoiding eye contact.

"Tell me, Mr. Kenner, how it is that we have nearly doubled profits at a time when most grand old estates are bleeding money?"

Kenner pushed his spectacles up his nose. "The farms, my lord, are doing quite well. Higgins has a generous arrangement with Simpson Textiles, making a tidy sum by providing the rapeseed oil they use to lubricate their machinery."

"Simpson Textiles? The factory over in Skipham? Managed by the American?"

"Owned by an American. The tycoon Orville Simpson. Yes, the very one. And Tilly Meadow is getting on well too, selling cheeses to markets throughout the countryside, and now Mrs. Cooper's baked goods as well—pies, cakes, and breads. Apparently, it has become dreadfully passé to bake one's own bread. Thornbrook Park profits on all ventures thanks to, er, having a hand in making the connections and drawing up the contracts."

"You? You drew up business contracts enabling the estate to share in the profits? Well done!" He had underestimated Kenner's cunning and skill. "But what's this about a guesthouse? There are an extraordinary number of notes on guesthouse profits."

"Oh." Kenner cleared his throat. "Indeed. Rather than allow the Dower House to just sit there empty…"

"Empty? What about Aunt Agatha? I've been meaning to mention that we need to move her out to make way for my mother's return, but has she already gone?"

"Your mother's return? The Dowager Countess is coming back?" Kenner sat up straighter, apparently on alert.

Gabriel nodded. "As soon as she's concluded her business in Paris, yes. Italy holds no enchantment for her since, well, since her romance with the Conte Miralini went sour. Poor Mother."

"Ah, I see. Agatha moved into the main house months ago to allow the Dower House to be rented to American guests."

"American guests? In the Dower House?" Gabriel tried to remain composed at the news, but in his astonishment, he felt his mouth gaping open like a trout on the line.

"I believe they're calling it a guesthouse, my lord. The visitors stay for a week or two to enjoy the charm of our fair countryside. We provide them a place to stay and a few meals in exchange for profits. A new couple arrived only days ago, a railroad man and his wife."

"A foreign couple is staying in the Dower House? How do you suddenly know so many Americans, Kenner?" Gabriel arched a brow. "It has to do with this new secretary of my wife's, doesn't it? I knew he would be trouble. Has he talked you into putting up his friends?"

Kenner shook his head. "They're not his friends. I believe they are associates of his former employer, and paying customers, as you can see."

"I can." Gabriel studied the ledger. "A tidy sum too. The illustrious Mrs. Belmont. How do Americans attract such wealth?"

"I'm afraid I've no idea."

"Ah, well, judging from the recent profits of the estate, you do have some idea. Tell me about this Grant fellow." Preparing for a more comfortable discussion, Gabriel swung his feet up to his desk, crossed his legs, and stretched out. His good old English boots were back on his feet, and he admired the well-worn yet sturdy sight of them.

"I would rather tell you myself, sir." A man appeared in his doorway. Tall. Broad-shouldered. Dark hair cropped short.

Gabriel dropped his feet back to the floor and stood to his full height. He kept his gaze narrowed and his hands clasped behind his back. It wouldn't do to hit the man on first acquaintance, even if Grant did strike the earl as a bounder. "Try 'my lord' or simply 'Lord Averford' if you must. You must be Grant."

"Grant, yes. Mr. Wesley Grant. Indeed, I am an American." The man stood ramrod straight, shoulders back, refusing to show that he could be cowed. Could he? "I must confess that it was your wife's idea to let the Dower House."

"My wife's idea?" Gabriel found he loathed hearing

about his wife from this arrogant stranger's lips. "What does Sophia know about guesthouses and such?"

"I suppose she concocted the idea after hearing about them from my former employer. When Mrs. Belmont visited, she suggested making a business of allowing Americans to experience the English countryside, fine as it is."

"It doesn't get any finer than here at Thornbrook Park," Gabriel agreed, hardly feeling appeased by the flattery.

"The Dower House was sitting there empty. Practically empty. There was the small matter of convincing Agatha to take a suite here. We've had no shortage of guests over the past eight months."

"She's been at it for eight months?" Again, Gabriel tried, and failed, to contain his surprise.

"We've been operating at full capacity. There's a waiting list."

"No shortage of Americans eager for the English experience?" Gabriel arched a brow.

"Willing to pay top dollar for the English experience. Mrs. Cooper at Tilly Meadow has been more than willing to supply the tarts, pastries, and cheese platters for afternoon tea." Grant stroked his square jaw as if pleased with pulling off a grand plan, placing into doubt how much of the enterprise Sophia had actually come up with and how much had been Grant's idea.

"Apple pie?" Gabriel took his seat and gestured for Grant to take the chair next to an apparently flummoxed Kenner. "With Mrs. Dennehy's cheddar? Mrs. Cooper makes the best apple pie."

Grant sucked in a breath. "I'm afraid not apple, my lord. Americans like to claim apple pie as their own. I've had her working with quince and currant, things that seem more English to American palates."

"Hmm." Gabriel nodded along, though he failed to understand how Americans could claim a pie filling as their own. "My mother is on her way home to Thornbrook Park, Grant. She's going to expect us to have her house ready. The Dower House. I can assure you that my wife won't want to be under the same roof as my mother."

"Be that as it may." Grant shrugged. What was it to him, the wrath of the Dowager Countess of Averford? "We have it reserved for the next six months."

"Six months?"

"Bringing in a tidy sum, my lord. Profits. Or I suppose you could always sell some land…"

Grant, the clever bastard, let his voice trail off suggestively. If the man knew anything about Thornbrook Park, he knew that selling land was not an option Gabriel cared to consider.

"You know quite a bit for a secretary, Grant. I daresay more than even Mr. Kenner seems to comprehend. Which one of you is going to inform me of the truth?"

"The truth, my lord?" Kenner pushed his spectacles up his nose again.

"Your loyalty to my wife is commendable, but even she wouldn't recommend that you endanger your positions by lying to me. I'll have the answers from her when she gets home, but I have things other than business I prefer to discuss with my wife. I can see that Lady Averford has been industrious in my absence. More ambitious than I imagined possible for her, if I'm being honest, and I'm impressed." More impressed than he cared to admit to his hired help.

Apparently, she'd taken a remarkable interest in the maintenance of Thornbrook Park. Was he to believe that she'd developed a keen sense of management affairs too? Or had Grant taken her under his wing? Or worse, in his arms. Gabriel closed his eyes tightly, eager to shut out the vision of Sophia in Lord Ralston's embrace that had haunted him for the past year. When he opened them again, he found Wesley Grant focused on him with an intent stare.

"Who are you really, Mr. Grant?" Gabriel asked, leaning forward. "Who are you to my wife?"

❧

The next morning, Sophia could not get home fast enough. In her head, she imagined her husband sitting down with Cornelius Kenner as Kenner stumbled through his answers, making his own incompetence more obvious with every word. Had Grant stepped in? Coached Kenner in her absence? Had Gabriel discovered her ruse? Could the train not go any faster? She knew she shouldn't worry about what she couldn't control, but right now her worrying was the very thing out of control. Thank goodness Mr. Dale was waiting for her at the station.

She tapped her foot impatiently as the chauffeur drove along at a snail's pace. Upon arrival, she didn't even wait for him to open her door. She flew out of the car and up the walk, leaving the man to handle her bags.

"Mr. Finch." He greeted her expectantly at the door, though he had failed to go out in time to meet her car. She handed him her hat and gloves. It was warm enough that she hadn't needed a coat. A bit too warm, actually, for June. "Where's my husband? In his study?"

Perhaps speaking to Mr. Kenner even now, discovering her deception, determining that he would divorce her…

"He's not here, Lady Averford. Perhaps he went shooting."

"Shooting? Next will be fishing and deer stalking. Home for a day and he's at it again!" She didn't stand a chance. Her husband was already up to his old activities. Anything but staying home alone with her.

"He couldn't bear to just wait for you. If you'll excuse me, he said that it didn't quite feel like home without you."

She felt her heart fluttering back to life, a wild bird in her chest. "He said that? He said Thornbrook Park was not home without me?"

"He did. I expect he will be back some time later."

"Later." Her spirit soared and then landed at her feet with a thud. Later. She had some time to prepare, to think how she would explain her actions. Or provide ample distractions. "Speak to Mrs. Mallows about preparing his favorite foods." His favorite foods were anything he could hunt or fish, of course. Meat he could kill with his own bare hands. "Or, whatever she has at the ready."

"Mrs. Mallows is already preparing, no doubt."

"Have Jenks see to my unpacking, and bring me some tea in the drawing room, please, Mr. Finch."

"Very good, my lady." Finch bowed.

"No, wait. It's a beautiful day." If a tad warm. "Forget the tea. I'll have some lemonade, and I'll take it on the terrace."

A while later, she had made it out past the terrace and all the way to the garden before the footman came carrying her lemonade on a tray with some of the Tilly Meadow cheese tarts she adored. He found her beside the arbor, examining the roses just beginning to bloom. "Just set it on the table there, Bill. Thank you."

Bill looked taken aback. Had she ever thanked him before? He placed the tray on the round wooden table near a chaise longue in the corner of the arbor, someone's private escape. Perhaps this was where Kenner ran off to when she couldn't find him in the house.

"Can I get you anything else, my lady?"

She shook her head. "Tell Finch not to be concerned if I don't hasten back inside. I plan to enjoy the outdoors."

Again, the footman's eyes widened in surprise. Lady Averford? Enjoying some time outdoors? It wasn't like her. Not at all. But the arbor provided cool shade and the birds were singing. The chaise longue at the edge of the grass looked like the perfect place to stretch out and plan what she would say to her husband. Or simply fall asleep, as it happened.

She woke some time later, disoriented until she glanced over at the dewy lemonade glass and what remained of her tarts after the birds had gotten to them. Sleep had done her a world of good. She couldn't remember the last time she'd slept so soundly.

The sun was low in the sky, and the birds had stopped their chirping, but there was a faint sound of music coming from across the orchard. A guitar? Someone not too far off strummed a guitar.

She rose to look around for the guitarist, pausing at the low wall to glimpse out beyond the garden. There in the distance, a man with a guitar walked toward the house. How odd!

He wore black trousers and a black jacket, something like a bolero, with a hat cocked at a jaunty angle on his head. Was he a troubadour, a wandering rogue? A pirate separated from the sea? He played with passion, his skilled fingers flying over the strings as he walked along. She'd never seen the likes of him in her quiet countryside, but her imagination went wild. Perhaps he was meeting a lover in the twilight. But the only one who seemed to be around to meet him was Sophia. And she had no lover. Not that her husband would ever believe it.

She peered into the increasing dimness, trying to make him out. Now she could see that he wore a billowy white shirt, open at the neck under his bolero, and his head was wrapped in a red silk scarf beneath his hat. She considered ducking around the corner of the wall to avoid being seen, but she couldn't take her eyes off him long enough to make her escape.

And as he closed the distance, he began to sing, his voice rich and low, rolling over the foreign words of his tune. Spanish? Italian? The song sounded sweet but tragic, and the apparent pain of his lyrics contorted his features so that she barely recognized him as he came closer and closer, stopping only inches from her on the other side of the wall.

"*Adesso che son priva dell' amore*," he sang. "*Abbasso gli occhi, e convien ch'io more, Adesso che son priva dal mio bene, Abbasso gl'occhi, e morir mi conviene!*"

She listened, enchanted, until the very end, when his voice hushed on the last word and he lowered his guitar.

"Greetings, signorina."

Her heart raced. It was all so unexpected. She was more than willing to play a part, drawing up to full height but keeping her eyes downcast, as if shy. "I'm sorry, sir. I don't know you. Allow me to get my husband…"

"Ah, this man, he is not at home." A statement, not a question.

"How would you know?" She met his gaze. Those soulful brown eyes. As if he could ever fool her. What was he trying to do? "He's at home, I tell you. And more men are not far off, tending my garden. No fewer than ten will come running to defend me if I scream."

He smiled, his lips full and soft and begging her to touch them. It had been so long. "But you won't scream, signorina. I trust you not to betray my secrets."

His accent remained strong and thick.

"Then you don't know me well. My own husband doesn't trust me."

In a swift bound, he leaped the low wall, causing her to shriek in surprise as he took her in his arms. "He is a fool. A fool not to trust you, a fool to leave you alone. Allow me to show you what it is to love."

He dipped her low, his lips hovering over hers.

Barely containing her laughter, she slipped a hand between their faces and tried to push him away. "Oh no, sir. As I've said, I don't know you. My kisses are only for my husband."

"Fool that he is?" He cocked a golden-blond brow.

"Fool that he is." She allowed herself to laugh at last, unable to keep her joy at seeing him bottled up any longer. He was home! And he was hers. Wasn't he?

"I'm glad to hear it." He laughed as well, the single dimple making its appearance in his left cheek. He only had a dimple on the one side. She'd always loved that one dimple when he smiled enough to bring it out, which wasn't often enough. At last, he released her and straightened up before pulling the hat and kerchief from his head. "My minstrel costume. I bought it in Italy. Do you see what I'm reduced to? Pulling a masquerade to get a kiss out of my own wife."

She reached for him, twining her fingers with his. "You don't have to act with me. I'm glad you're back, Gabriel. I've missed you."

He studied her as if uncertain. "Honestly? After I ran off and left you on your own?"

"You had your reasons." She hadn't been blameless, and yet it seemed that they could put it all behind them at last. She brought his hand to her lips and kissed it, savoring the warmth of him, the softness, the rugged scent of leather and tobacco. Had he taken up smoking, or was it all for the part he played?

He closed his eyes, possibly also savoring the feel of her next to him after such a long separation.

"What was the song? You've perfected your Italian.

It certainly wasn't your accent that gave you away." For all she'd agonized over what to say when she was with him again, words came easily between them, and she was glad.

"An Italian folk song," he said. "'C'era Una Volta.' In English, 'There Was a Time.' It's about love and loss and the agony a lover feels upon his abandonment."

Had he been in agony too? "The agony is that we never talked about it, Gabriel. You just…left."

"I left. But you can't deny pushing me away. I no longer knew if you even wanted me." After seeing her with another man. She was grateful that he didn't say it out loud. Instead, he took her in his arms and held her so close that she couldn't help but look up at him to see the genuine pain in his eyes. "Tell me," he said. "Can we find our way back to each other? Do you even want to try?"

"Of course I do. I want you, Gabriel. I want—"

She didn't complete her thought before his lips came down on hers, insistent, fierce, nearly crushing, then soft and light as a whispered plea. She opened her mouth to him, drawing him into her, her tongue curling with his, laving him until she felt quite dizzy in his arms and the familiar flames of passion licked at her core.

Breathless, she broke the kiss and leaned against him, her head resting on his solid chest where she could feel the rapid beating of his heart. "Gabriel."

"Sophia." He stroked her hair. "My beautiful wife."

"You didn't go shooting after all. You were waiting to surprise me." She looked up at him.

"Why would I go shooting when you were on your

way back to me? I mean to stay here with you where I belong. If you'll have me. I understand you've become quite possessive of the place."

She drew back from him. "Where did you hear such a thing?"

"From Kenner. And Mr. Grant. I know all about what you've been up to while I've been gone."

"All? They gave me up so easily?" Her most loyal servants, or so she'd thought.

"With their jobs on the line? Of course they did. They told me everything. I'm impressed, really. I never thought you had it in you, Sophia."

"You threatened them?" No, he didn't think she had it in her, did he? And that was at the heart of their problems, not so easily solved with his return after all. "Never? You never believed me capable of running your precious estate? Vapid, beautiful Sophia. She looks good on my arm, but I wouldn't trust her to function without guidance."

"It's not a fault of yours, darling. Women aren't created to deal with business affairs." His fingers curled on her shoulder. She yanked away, arms crossed. "You should have better things to think about, and now that I'm home…"

"Now that you're home, I don't have to worry my pretty head? Typical male misconceptions. What are women made for? Your pleasure? Bearing your young?" She turned away to conceal the tears hovering on the brink, the pain of their loss still too raw. "I've found great enjoyment in business affairs. You've never believed in me, Gabriel. Have you ever really known me at all?"

"I—" He paused before going on the defensive. "Maybe not. Fair enough. I fell in love at the first sight of you, your beauty, your charm."

"My figure." She'd always had an enviable figure, tall and elegant, graceful. Pert breasts, narrow waist. Even when she was a girl, just old enough to attend her first ball, she knew what men wanted when they looked at her. Inevitably, they would try to dance her out to a terrace or a quiet corner and attempt to kiss her. Gabriel alone had been a mystery to her, at first. He'd looked at her like he wanted what the others had wanted, but he hadn't tried to get her alone. He didn't kiss her until she practically begged. And even then, he'd asked her permission first.

"May I kiss you?" She'd thought him silly and old-fashioned.

"Yes, your figure," the present-day Gabriel agreed readily enough, his eyes settling on the curve of her waist nipped in by her ivory blouse tucked into a slim-fitting blue skirt.

Perhaps he imagined the corset beneath her clothes. Designed to serve a purpose, it was unadorned by lace and of an inconsequential gray, yet still perhaps enough to drive him mad to think of it against her skin, holding her intimately as she longed for him to do. Even after a nap, Sophia fancied herself impeccably put together as always, but how she longed for him to be the one to slowly pull her apart.

He breached the distance she had put between them and dared to slide his hand under the soft point of her chin, tipping her face up to look at him. "I knew that you were the one I wanted to marry, and I planned to convince you at all costs. Somewhere along the way, I failed to realize that keeping you was worth the effort it took to win you over in the first place. I failed. I failed to show you what you mean to me every day. Every hour."

"I failed as well." She uncrossed her arms and shrugged. How hard it must have been for him to admit a shortcoming, and she cherished his candor. Still, she couldn't let him accept all of the blame. "I failed to tell you what I needed and how your negligence hurt me."

He tipped his head. "I wouldn't exactly say 'negligence.'"

"Negligence." She clung to the word. It was the right one. And she'd learned to be too sure of herself to back down. "It's about time that you discover I have a sharp mind too. A rather clever one. With a surprising penchant for business."

For years, she'd failed to understand Alice's and Eve's demands for respect and rights for women. What was wrong with letting men run the world? Now that she'd had a taste of managing on her own, she knew exactly why they were always so insistent on progress and equality. Women were every bit as capable as men. England had been successfully ruled by queens, no less! Who could doubt women after that?

"With Mr. Grant's help," Gabriel added, as if he couldn't help himself, stealing away at the credit she'd earned.

"The smartest men surround themselves with good help. You've always said so."

"True." He nodded. "Clearly, I have a lot to work on. We both do."

"Both?"

"You work on letting me get to know you better. I'll work on being the man you need me to be. I've changed, Sophia. Italy has changed me."

"I've changed too. Being in a position of power has changed me. You'll find me a formidable force, Lord Averford. I do hope you're up for a challenge."

His mouth curved into a crooked grin, an expression she hardly recognized on him. "I'm up for anything you can dish out, *cara mia*."

Four

WERE THEY FRIENDS OR ENEMIES? GABRIEL COULDN'T tell. His homecoming hadn't gone off exactly as he'd planned. In his imagined version of events, his singing won her over instantly. There were no words or questions between them. He simply set down the guitar, swept her swooning into his arms, and made mad, passionate love to her. Why had he made the mistake of talking? Talking always led to uncertainty.

He refrained from saying more as he led her back inside, his hand at the small of her back. Dare he drop it lower? One small caress to the curve of her backside? Or would she slap him? Too soon? He glanced at her pert, luscious curves, which tempted him from under the white linen skirt that clung admirably to her frame. She'd always had an incredible figure...

"Gabriel." Her tone reflected her surprise and perhaps just the barest hint of a reprimand.

"What? I've missed you." His hand acted before his mind could stop it, smoothing over the back of her skirt to cup the firm mound of her derriere. As long as she hadn't slapped him, he figured he might as well brazen it out. "You are my wife."

"I am. I hope you remembered that as well in Italy as you do now that you've returned." She flashed him a smug grin and increased her pace to escape him, taking the lead.

He ran to catch up, turning so that he faced her even though he risked tripping over a stone as he continued on backward. "I could never forget. You were on my mind constantly. You and no other."

"It would have been difficult to become a lothario when you were staying with your mother, I suppose, though not impossible."

"Speaking of Mother…" He had to warn Sophia of his mother's impending return, but he dreaded how she would take the news.

"No, let's not. I can't imagine any good reason to bring her into the conversation. I'm sorry I mentioned her at all."

With his mother still in France, he supposed he could wait for a more opportune time to tell Sophia of their need to clear their guests out of the Dower House. Mother always took weeks to shop her way through Paris. "Let's speak of brighter things. Dinner. Just the two of us. Perhaps we could even dismiss all the servants. Give them the night off."

"When you've just returned?" She pursed her lips in the way that signaled her annoyance, a gesture he remembered all too well. And how he'd missed it! "Who do you expect will serve if we dismiss the servants? You imagine I'll fawn over you simply because you've come back."

He wouldn't mind a little fawning. "Of course not. I'll serve you."

She shook her head. "Better to concentrate on making up to me, don't you think? You haven't the faintest idea what goes into serving a meal."

"Don't I? Ah, there's where you're mistaken. I've learned a great many things during my time away, including how to cook and serve a meal. Now you're guilty of underestimating me as well. It seems we both have work to do in getting reacquainted."

"You cook?" Her mouth gaped the slightest bit. "Wonders never cease. I would like to experience a meal cooked and served by you. It can't be today, I'm afraid. The servants must be all too happy to have you home to allow us the indulgence of insisting they stay out of our way."

Sophia, concerned for the servants? He laced his fingers with hers. "They're excited to see us together again. Let's give them the show they're expecting, shall we?"

"What kind of show?" She arched a thin, black brow.

"A romantic one, of course. They want the reassurance of knowing that all is right in our world."

She nodded. "So that there's no uncertainty that all is right with theirs. We do set the tone, don't we?"

"We do. You've always said so." Reassured that they were of one mind, he released her hand to place his arm around her. She leaned comfortably into him. This. This closeness. What he'd missed the most was feeling intimately close to another human being. To Sophia. "But one thing. Do we have to allow that Grant man to join us at dinner? And Agatha. I would rather it be the two of us alone."

"'That Grant man'? Are you jealous, Gabriel? I assure you…"

"No need to reassure me, darling. I trust you. Completely." Did he? "It's just that he's the sort of man who looks like he would be appealing to the ladies, although I know you value his opinion."

"I do. He's got remarkable sense. But I'm not attracted to him. Just the same, it means the world to hear you say that you trust me. It's a good start."

Friends then, he decided. They were to be friends, not enemies. Lovers? That might take more convincing. But it was indeed a good start.

❧

Safe in her room, Sophia leaned against the door to catch her breath. Kissing him had put her in mind for other things. And when he'd placed his hands on her, cupping her bottom, she'd nearly melted on the spot. She could not afford to lose her mind. Not with so much left to clear up between them.

Her husband might be ready to fight for the rights of all men in Parliament, but he was clearly still against the rights of women. Believing her to be out of her element in business because she wore skirts? Ridiculous. After seeing the ledger, irrefutable proof of her success, Gabriel still seemed to require more proof that his wife had managed Thornbrook Park every bit as well as he had, perhaps even better.

He had learned to cook. She wondered what other skills he had picked up during his adventures. They had much to learn about one another, but she'd insisted they part to get ready for dinner. If they resumed sharing a room too soon, they might regret it. Better to keep some mystery between them for now. Besides, Gabriel's valet would enjoy the chance to catch up with him too.

Burns had been restless without his lord at home. Sophia hadn't had the heart to fire him. It would have been like admitting her uncertainty that her husband was ever coming back. Instead, she'd allowed him to look after Mr. Grant and any other visiting gentlemen. The Thornes visited frequently and sometimes stayed for days. He'd had no shortage of work despite Gabriel's absence, but now Burns could look after Gabriel exclusively. From now on, Mr. Grant and Marcus would have to rely on a footman's assistance.

"I suspect you'll be wanting the new Worth?" Jenks asked, emerging from the closet, gown in hand. It was a gorgeous creation, a hand-beaded silk in a blue several shades deeper than Sophia's eyes.

"Exactly what I had in mind. Thank you, Jenks. You're a dear. Jean-Philippe always knows exactly what will suit a woman best."

Jenks flashed her tight-lipped grin. "I'll go run your bath."

Sophia couldn't help but think about how well Jenks would look on Wesley Grant's arm, but some of her most egregious affronts to friends and family had been through her well-intentioned matchmaking. She wouldn't dare attempt it again. If her maid and estate agent were suited, they would just have to find their way to each other without her intervention.

"Oh, I forgot to mention." Having gone to start the bath, Jenks peered around the door. "Aunt Agatha sent word that she is taking dinner on a tray in her room. Something about improving her communications with the spirit world."

Sophia made a ghastly face and wiggled her fingers in the air. "I'm sensing a disturbance…"

Jenks laughed politely, and Sophia realized her slip, making fun at her aunt's expense in front of the servants. What had come over her? "I believe she's simply being generous," Sophia said, by way of correcting her flub. "Giving Gabriel and me some time alone now that he is home."

"I agree." Jenks reemerged and pulled Sophia's robe from the closet. "She's perceptive, if anything, and so kind."

Sophia felt all the more admonished. "The kindest. What would I have done all these months without her?"

"She relies on you too. And Miss Puss, of course."

Sophia suspected Jenks had added that last bit so that Sophia wouldn't be the only one having a little fun with Agatha. "Let's not forget Miss Puss."

With Jenks's help, she slipped out of her clothes into her robe and headed to the waiting bath. Once in, relishing the feel of the warm water and the smell of lavender, Sophia called Jenks back.

"Jenks? I just want to thank you for all that you do. You're a tremendous help to me every day, and I'm sorry if I haven't said it enough." Or at all.

Jenks appeared taken aback. "Nonsense. It's my job, Lady Averford. I'm happy to do it, and I strive to do it well. 'Do your best, or what's the point,' my severe old nana always said."

"She would be proud of you, Jenks."

Jenks shook her head, a wide smile—not the tight-lipped one—on her face. "Pardon me for speaking out, but what has gotten into you? Making jokes, thanking the servants? What next? Are you going to start giving us all gifts? Are you feeling well, Lady Averford?"

Sophia laughed. "I'm perfectly well, thank you. I suppose I've learned to be more appreciative of all that I have after nearly losing…" Her voice broke off and she realized her laughter had made way for tears. Big drops. Falling into the tub. She couldn't stop them. "Well, I'm grateful. Time to start showing it more."

"Oh now, don't cry. Or go ahead. Have a good cry. Sometimes we need to cry it out, don't we?" She brought Sophia a towel and remained poised at the edge of the tub. "You're in the right place for it. If we'd already gotten you dressed, we might have to change to a dry gown before dinner."

"Wouldn't that be a sight? The countess showing emotion after years of remaining aloof? Someone might get the idea that I'm human after all."

"You are human. A title doesn't change that. And you're a good woman, if I may say so, Lady Averford. Everyone in the house thinks very highly of you."

"Good of you to say, Jenks." Perhaps everyone but the housekeeper, Mrs. Hoyle. Sophia dried her eyes on the edge of the towel. "I thought everyone was against me when I first came to Thornbrook Park and the Dowager Countess ruled all. But when she left, and some of the old servants left with her, I felt I had a chance."

"I don't know about her," Jenks said, standing and

making her way back to the door. Probably eager to escape… "Never met her. But I do know you. You hired me and you've always been good to me. I'm grateful too, for my job and a good place in this beautiful house."

"It is beautiful, isn't it?"

"Grand. Now keep in mind I might still be thinking of gifts." Jenks laughed. "I've always loved your diamond cuff bracelet, if you should ever consider parting with it."

Sophia was glad for Jenks's good humor, which was pulling her out of the abyss. "You know I'll never part with that one. It was a gift."

"From your husband. I know. Now finish your bath so we have time to dress you up and do your great beauty justice. The earl needs to see just what he's been missing by staying away so long."

A short time later, Sophia glided down the stairs refreshed and feeling pretty. Jenks had worked her usual magic in pinning her hair at her nape, with soft strands falling to frame her face in perfectly planned "escape" from her diamond comb. The beading of her gown picked up the low light, shimmering as she crossed the drawing room.

"Champagne?" Her breath caught at the sight of her handsome husband awaiting her, two glasses in hand. She hadn't exactly forgotten how well he filled out a tuxedo, but she couldn't help but feel the fresh tingles running through her blood like bubbles in the champagne when she looked him over. Golden-blond hair just brushing the top of his dark collar, tanned skin. Apparently he'd spent a lot of time outdoors in

Italy. His shoulders were broad enough to carry the weight of the world, or at least all of Thornbrook Park.

"It's appropriate for tonight." He handed her a glass and held her gaze, his coffee eyes aglow. "A celebration. I'm so happy to be home. Happiest to be with you, my exquisite wife."

She clinked her glass to his. "To your return. I'd almost forgotten how suited you are to dressing up, for a man who prefers the out-of-doors."

His full lips parted in a smile, bringing out the single dimple in his left cheek. "I've a new interest in interiors."

"Oh? So you won't be getting up at the break of dawn to go out and kill some poor unsuspecting animal?"

"Some poor unsuspecting animal will be gracing our table tonight, and thank goodness for it. The Italians offer some interesting cuisine, but there's nothing like a good English roasted haunch."

"A haunch? You make it sound so appetizing. Not exactly what you learned to cook in Italy then, I presume."

"I learned to make gnocchi, little Italian potato dumplings, served with sage in a butter sauce. And risotto. I've perfected my risotto, or so our cook, Signora Gugino, told me. She was my instructor. Some mornings, I would help her go out and look for mushrooms. She taught me which ones were good for eating and which to avoid."

"My husband, the mushroom hunter? Astounding."

"I can show you. We have a few of the same kind growing in the woods here."

"I would like that." She took a long sip of champagne. "And your risotto, or the neo-key, what did you call it?"

"Gnocchi. Soon. We'll have a big Italian feast just as soon as Mrs. Mallows allows me to take over her kitchen." Surprising her, he pulled Sophia to him, his arm curling around her waist and placing her body in front of his. With his free hand, he lifted his glass to her portrait, his lips less than an inch from her ear as he whispered. "We'll have to order a new portrait painted, or perhaps a photograph, which is more likely to capture your real beauty. You've only grown more stunning since this one was hung."

She didn't want to remind him that he'd barely noticed when her new portrait was hung, replacing the one of his mother that had been there for twenty years or more. Instead, she leaned against him, enjoying the feel of his solidity against her, his arm around her, his fingers spreading possessively over her abdomen. She closed her eyes, savoring their intimacy. Was that… Yes, she believed he was becoming even more solid against her backside. It was only natural, she supposed, after so much time apart, but…he wanted her. She thrilled deep inside. He still wanted her. They remained standing, looking at her portrait, neither one willing to move and break the spell. Dinner? She didn't care if she ever ate again so long as he loved her.

Do you love me, Gabriel? She would have turned in his arms to ask if she wasn't so afraid of the answer. Did he know her enough to love her? For that matter, did she know him, this man who sang ballads and cooked dishes she couldn't pronounce properly and foraged for mushrooms? Still, it wouldn't hurt to ask. To talk. They wouldn't learn a thing about each other if they only relied on their bodies to relay information. Lust wasn't love. Not entirely. Though some of that wouldn't hurt to bring them together either.

The first night he'd made love to her, he had brought her to a whole new world. It was as if she hadn't really opened her eyes, heard, smelled, touched, or existed before he'd made her quiver under his touch. And she hadn't been able to control herself when he replaced his fingers with his tongue, sending tremor after tremor through her until her nerves were raw with pleasure and she couldn't remember her own name. She'd managed to call out his name though, so loudly she was surprised all the servants hadn't come running. Oh, that first night.

But the shame that followed in the morning, when she remembered her mother's warning: "Men want a lady to set the example in the bedroom of someone who will bear their young and keep their house. When they want whores, they know where to find them. Act like a whore, and he will begin to treat you like one."

Under no circumstances was she to show her husband that she enjoyed the things he did to her body, her mother had told her on her wedding night. Mother sounded as if she found it hard to believe that anyone could enjoy any of it, but she was covering all territory in case.

Sophia wasn't sure she believed Mother. What was the harm? She had liked what Gabriel did to her. She wanted more of it. And she certainly didn't want her husband running off to do such things to a whore. To anyone else! No one but her, his own wife. Perhaps she could enjoy it more quietly, she'd told herself, a compromise.

He could keep making love to her, and she could pretend that she was a lady and recognized it as her duty but also like it a little, just not enough to scream and beg and cry. And so they went on until the day he tried to turn her around and take her from behind, the thing her mother had warned her most about— doing things that men would only expect a whore and not a wife to do, things like taking him in her mouth or allowing him to mount her like an animal (her mother's own words). Mother had gone over a list.

But when he'd gripped her so roughly and spun her around, heaven help her! She'd never wanted him more. Perhaps she was more whore than lady, deep down. Perhaps she'd shown him that he could treat her like a whore. She had no one to ask. A younger sister? Alice wouldn't know. Mother hadn't even given Alice the talk yet. Aunt Agatha? No, Sophia couldn't even imagine bringing it up.

Her best friend, Eve, in India? No, it would take forever to get the letters back and forth, and would she even be able to write such things down? That left only her mother-in-law, her husband's mother, and what might she think of Sophia asking such questions? Fortunately, Sophia had fallen pregnant, and that had put an end to their relations for a time.

Now a grown woman and no longer a girl, she knew that desiring her husband did not make her a whore. She knew a great many things more than she had back then—from experience, reading books, and talking to friends. She'd learned from Eve that Eve and Marcus had even kept up relations all through Eve's pregnancies.

A year into their marriage, Gabriel must have been as confused as she was when she'd started to become more prim instead of more adventurous. And then after Edward's death? She was so afraid to go through it all again. But with Gabriel's proximity, the familiar feelings were rising inside her, and the need, wild and powerful, was clawing like a beast inside her, dying to get out.

"I suppose it's time we go in to dinner." His hoarse voice broke the silence and the mood, just as she'd been about to turn and forget all words, to throw herself into his arms and beg for him.

She wanted him to be the one to beg, she reminded herself. "Yes, dinner. Let's get you some of that haunch you're craving."

Turning with a smile, she captured his gaze again. She saw hunger there, but not for venison or beef. Maybe after dinner, if she flirted and allowed him to glimpse her cleavage, he would admit to wanting her, missing her, needing her desperately...

Mr. Finch appeared in the doorway, a blond head bobbing behind him, a woman's and then a man's voice calling out, one or two visitors desperate to get by before being properly announced. Who? She wanted to instruct Finch to send them away, but it would be rude with them standing right there. And then it happened. The thing she had been dreading for the past six years. She froze.

"Your mother, my lord. The Dowager Countess of Averford has arrived to see you."

Five

UNSURPRISINGLY, GABRIEL'S MOTHER DIDN'T WAIT FOR the proper greeting. She pushed right by Finch and took the room by storm. All the hope that had been building inside Gabriel, the dream of a night alone with his wife, turned to ashes when he saw his wife's eyes widen with alarm at the sight of his mother.

"Not just a visit, my darlings. I'm home. Home to stay!" His mother threw open her arms and ran at him, enfolding him in a brief embrace before moving on to Sophia. The Dowager Countess knew enough to not embrace Sophia, but worse, she reached out and patted her cheeks instead. "Look at you!"

Sophia blinked, her mouth remaining open in shock or horror. Shocked horror.

"Emotion, Gabe! I believe your coolly polite wife is showing emotion! Close your mouth, dear. It's not a dream. I'm really here. Why didn't you tell her I was coming?"

Sophia turned to him, blue eyes blazing. "You knew? You knew your mother's arrival was imminent, and you didn't say anything?"

"I... Forgive me, I tried. You didn't want to discuss her. And I hardly knew she was coming so soon. I knew she was in Paris, yes, but..."

"Paris was a mistake." Mother waved her arms dramatically. "Not entirely. I did choose some lovely gowns, but I decided not to wait for them. Jean-Philippe will have them sent here, of course. Do you know that my measurements are exactly what they were twenty years ago when Charles Frederick first took them?" She posed, hands on hips, then gestured to Sophia's frock. "A Worth?"

"Yes, it is. House of Worth." Sophia wouldn't say more than necessary. Gabriel was surprised that she'd regained her power of speech in time to answer.

"She always had taste," Mother said dismissively, her attention drawn to Sophia's portrait above the fireplace. She scowled, but the man who had come in quietly after her cleared his throat, drawing their attention.

"Lord Markham?" It was Gabriel's turn to be surprised. "What are you doing here? Come in, of course. Make yourself at home. You still know the place well enough, I imagine."

"He accompanied me on the train!" Mother spoke in exclamations, revealing to Gabriel that she had already been drinking. She always got loud when drinking. "The dear man! And then to the Dower House, where we met the loveliest couple. Americans! Living in my house! Did you know?"

Gabriel nodded.

"We visited with them for some time. Didn't we, Charlie boy? Great fun. They do like their whiskey, the Americans."

"It appears you have a taste for it too." Gabriel shouldn't have been so indelicate, but he could hardly contain himself in his anger at her sudden appearance before he could warn Sophia, and just as things were going so well…

"My fault, I'm afraid." Lord Markham stepped forward. "She admitted to being nervous on the train, and I suggested a drink might calm her down."

"Mother, nervous?" Gabriel stared at Markham as if the man had grown a second head.

"Hard to imagine, isn't it?" Mother winked at Lord Markham. Winked! Had she been leading the poor man on all afternoon? In his sensitive state following the divorce? Gabriel could not forget that Markham had held an attraction for Mother once upon a time, before she'd married Gabriel's father. "But yes, I was nervous. I haven't been back in so long. And then there was Charles, and we started talking and discovered we were headed in the same direction."

"Your lovely wife invited me," Markham informed Gabriel before turning to Sophia. "Thank you, Sophia. I hope it's not too soon. I've been so lonely in London."

She hesitated. "I did say that you were welcome to come and see us, Charles. Of course." If his wife, the consummate hostess, felt any annoyance at Markham's presence, she didn't show it. But then, her cheeks remained red from her shock at seeing Mother.

"Charles? And Sophia? When did the two of you become so close?" Gabriel's gaze flitted between them from one to the other. He was almost afraid he might catch them sharing a conspiratorial smile or intimate gesture.

"We've all been friends for so long," Sophia explained. "When I came to find you in London, I met Charles at Averford House. He'd stopped in to whisk you away to the pub, and I asked him to stay for dinner. It only seemed natural to drop all formality."

"And the dear girl offered this drowning old man a lifeline with her invitation. I'll forever be grateful." Markham bowed in Sophia's direction. "And then, of course, I had the good fortune of finding Teresa on the train."

Teresa, Mother's given name. So they were all to be an intimate party sharing a jolly, old respite at Thornbrook Park, were they? Gabriel could hardly resent Markham, the poor man, for attempting to distract himself in his time of grief for a crumbled marriage. But Gabriel had his own marriage to think about, his own wife, and how he wanted her all to himself.

"I might as well send word to Aunt Agatha to join us," Sophia said. "If we're to be a group instead of just a pair." When she met Gabriel's gaze, she revealed more than she expected, he imagined. He could see the regret clouding her eyes. He wasn't the only one disappointed in the turn of events, but it was little consolation to think of them both being miserable.

"Yes, send for her. She does liven up any affair." At least he could say that for Agatha, that she knew how to keep things exciting with her spirit talk and fortune-telling. "I missed her too, as it happens."

"We'll have a merry bunch indeed," Mother said,

gesturing for Finch to cross the room and pour her some champagne. "The Americans will be joining us too."

"The Americans?" Both Gabriel and Sophia turned at once to face Mother.

"The ones in my house, yes. The Waldens. Very lovely couple. He's a railroad tycoon, and she's from a newspaper family. They're friends with the Belmonts, apparently. You know Alva and her special projects—first suffrage, now organizing tours abroad."

"Yes." Sophia set her glass down, apparently finished after only a few sips. "That's how they were recommended to us, through our estate agent who was formerly employed by Mrs. Belmont, Alva."

If Gabriel remembered correctly, Sophia couldn't stand Alva Belmont's daughter, the Duchess of Marlborough, for sweeping into London and stealing all the young men's hearts before Sophia had been about to make her own debut. Consuelo Vanderbilt was all the men could speak of that year. Quite a few of Gabriel's own school friends were head over heels for her, even though she was already promised to the duke.

"Imagine my surprise when I arrived at home to find it occupied. We all had a good laugh, and I invited them here for dinner. If you're interested in fine English country living, I told them, you'll find no better example than at Thornbrook Park. A wonder you didn't put them up here. You have the rooms."

"The Dower House is large enough and offered more privacy for them."

"And for you. No matter, dear. I've arranged for

my things to be brought over here and unpacked. I gave myself the blue room. It will do for now. Mrs. Hoyle is preparing everything. The Americans can stay in my house. And how lovely to have someone to entertain! It can get so quiet here in the country."

Somehow, his wife managed not to flinch at the news. Sophia liked it quiet. She preferred to rule over their own small group of friends and acquaintances, people she knew well enough to not have to guess their preferences and dislikes. And he wished his mother would remember that the Dower House wasn't hers exactly, though he would hardly deny his own mother the right to stay there.

"Charles, has Mr. Finch sent a footman to see to your things?" Sophia was about to gesture for Finch, but Mother stepped in again.

"Of course. I'm putting him in the green room next to mine."

"That will never do," Sophia said. "The green room and the two next to it are always reserved for the Thornes. Mina and Freddie need their space, and of course there's the nurse…"

"Freddie?" Mother crinkled her nose. "You've taken to calling Winifred by a boy's name?"

Sophia shrugged. "Her parents have, and I always respect their wishes. Besides, I think it suits her. Perhaps you'll agree with me when you meet her."

"What's that supposed to mean? Does she dress like a boy? Heavens, has Marcus's desire to have a son taken his last shred of sense?"

"Actually, she's a very feminine baby. But what does it matter?" Marcus seemed perfectly content with his girls, at any rate. Not that Gabriel would argue further with his mother if avoidable.

"Alva Belmont would probably agree with you. She argues with anyone over rights for women. She stayed with us in Italy for weeks, speaking of nothing but rights."

"You don't agree with her? You don't think we should have rights, Teresa?" Teresa. His wife had taken to calling his mother by her first name. He felt his breath catch, wondering how Mother would bear it.

She didn't blink. "We should have rights, but no need to be so strident about it. It's unladylike." Mother tipped her glass up and downed all her champagne in one gulp.

"Mustn't be unladylike. The horror." Gabriel flashed a grin at Markham just as Finch stepped in to introduce the Americans.

"Mr. and Mrs. Walden." Finch showed them in and took Sophia aside. Gabriel could overhear the butler reassuring his wife that he had used his own judgment and instructed a footman to set Lord Markham up in an east-wing bedroom.

Sophia, seemingly pleased, rejoined them in time for more personal introductions before going in to dinner.

"My word, what an impressive portrait." Mrs. Walden, a short woman with wild red curls barely contained in a bun at the back of her head, endeared herself to Sophia right away with the recognition. "Perhaps you'll share the name of your artist so I can have one like it of myself."

"I'll write it down for you after dinner." Sophia reached out to pat the woman's hand, a kind of spontaneously friendly gesture Gabriel had never seen her make before. "Do you like champagne? We've opened a bottle."

"Yes, quite a likeness," Mother observed, seemingly put out at having to share the Americans now that she'd invited them. Gabriel braced himself. "Though of course some time has passed. You look a bit older now, especially around the eyes. I suppose you replaced my portrait as soon as you could."

"I only had it done last year," Sophia said.

"Oh." Mother pursed her lips. "Forgive me then. But I suppose aging is inevitable for us all. Which reminds me… Charles was telling me quite the story on the train. How I laughed!"

"What story?" Sophia asked. But clearly she had an idea, because Gabriel watched her eyes flash daggers at Charles, who colored under her scrutiny.

"About Lord Wilkerson confusing you for me. Can you imagine? We're nothing alike."

"Nothing at all," Sophia agreed. "He wasn't wearing his spectacles."

"Ah, that explains it." Gabriel reached for his wife's arm and tucked it into his elbow. "The man can't see a thing without his spectacles. Mother, keep that in mind if he ever comes to call. You'll look as young as my fair bride to Wilkerson as long as he forgets his eyeglasses."

Mother harrumphed loudly. Just when Gabriel supposed things were about to take an unfortunate turn, he watched Aunt Agatha sweep in on Mr. Grant's arm.

"I hope we're not too late. I'd planned on taking dinner in my room, but Miss Puss nudged me to the door, as she does when we're having a party. I sent word asking Mr. Grant to be kind enough to escort me. I hate to show up to a party unattended." Agatha, in her crimson and gold ensemble, beamed up at Grant like a lovesick schoolgirl. Would wonders never cease?

"Mr. Grant, you say?" Catching the scent of fresh prey, Mother crossed the room to the newcomers. "The tycoon?"

"The estate agent." Sophia, standing nearby, was all too happy to correct the Dowager Countess. "Mr. Grant came highly recommended by Alva Belmont."

"In fact, the countess lured me away. I'm pleased to make your acquaintance, Lady Averford. I've heard so much about you." Grant cast a conspiratorial glance at Sophia.

Mother's gaze darted back and forth between the two of them. "I'm sure you have. With me tucked away in Italy, there's a certain freedom from reproach."

"On the contrary, I've always admired how the countess holds you in such high esteem. To move heaven and earth to make sure the house would always stand at the ready in the event of your unheralded return shows no shortage of regard. 'The dower house is no place for my mother-in-law,' she always says. 'She belongs here with her family.' And here you are."

With one blond brow raised, Mother couldn't hide her astonishment and perhaps a fair amount of skepticism at Grant's words. Gabriel believed Grant could rival his brother, Marcus, for a quick wit and unshakeable charm.

Seemingly convinced of the authenticity of Grant's report, Mother took the man's arm and led him away from Sophia. "Perhaps you can tell me where she has stored my portrait…"

Without another thought to the rest of them, Mother started toward the dining room with Mr. Grant.

"Shall we, then?" Gabriel offered his arm to his wife, knowing the others would follow them in for dinner. "She's temporarily diverted," he said for Sophia's ears alone. "Perhaps long enough for her to regain her bearings."

"I'm not sure that I don't prefer her without her bearings, completely adrift. But she obviously has some command of herself. She made sure that she got to go in first, before her host and hostess. She'll put herself in charge of our great estate just as soon as she can and make sure the rest of us all answer to her."

"I doubt you'll allow it to happen, darling, now that you've established yourself as a force." He cast her a sidelong glance.

"I wouldn't say that I'm a force." She smiled in his direction as he'd hoped she would.

"Your minion was prepared to do your bidding. Look how fast he stepped in to smooth things over with Mother."

"My minion? Mr. Grant? Are you suggesting I'm some sort of a villain? A witch from the fairy tales perhaps?"

Gabriel shuddered at his own stupidity. It wasn't the impression he'd meant to invoke. "Not at all. But he does seem fiercely loyal to you."

"Not loyal enough to spare any details of my command under questioning by the enemy."

Her words cut him deeply and caught him unprepared. "Your enemy? Tell me it hasn't come to that. Please, Sophia." He gripped her by the wrist so that she had to turn to face him. "I couldn't bear it."

Her eyes softened as she soon as she met his gaze. "Of course not, Gabriel. Up until this afternoon, I wasn't sure. But we're not enemies. I know it now."

She didn't exactly clarify what they were to each other, if not enemies. Gabriel supposed that she had as much idea of how to define their relationship as he had.

&⌣⌢

Dinner went wonderfully as always, the Earl and Countess of Averford playing their roles to perfection. While they were seated at the table, it was just another night at Thornbrook Park, another of their celebrated dinners, and not a momentous occasion in which Gabriel and Sophia stumbled over what to say to each other after finally reuniting following a bitter year apart.

Conversation flowed more readily than the wine that well-trained footmen replenished before the gilt-edged crystal goblets could even be emptied. Sophia took a liking to their American guests, so much so that she stopped thinking of them as Americans and began to think of them as friends. How they chattered on about this, that, and everything that struck their fancy! Even the Dowager Countess could barely fit a word in edgewise.

The awkward silence would settle between them

later, Sophia supposed. Once the guests were gone. Though Gabriel's mother would remain, as well as Lord Markham, Aunt Agatha, Mr. Grant, and the countless servants who filled their house. They could put off ever finding themselves alone together again, should they choose to do so.

But Sophia found that she wanted to be alone with Gabriel. Desperately. She studied him over cordials after dinner in the drawing room. He always held extraordinary command over a room, his mere presence drawing attention. It helped that he was taller than most men of their acquaintance, Sophia supposed. And he had those naturally broad shoulders. Those soulful, brooding brown eyes could turn to weapons in an instant, piercing straight through to one's soul to lay all secrets bare. She thrilled at the very idea of being laid bare by Gabriel. *Take me, Husband. Take me now!* Surely they could find a quiet nook away from their guests. With the Americans yammering on, who would notice?

She smiled at the idea and rejoined the conversation. It wouldn't do for the hostess to be woolgathering off in a corner, especially not with Gabriel's mother all too ready to step in and resume the role she clearly believed to be hers by right. Sophia could see the way Teresa looked around the room, likely imagining how things used to be and how she could manage to set them all back to rights.

"Newport sounds lovely," Sophia said after Louise Walden finished describing their "cottage" by the sea. It sounded more like a palace, but perhaps Sophia hadn't been paying proper attention.

"Only when Alva Belmont's out of town, to be sure." Teresa held her empty cordial glass aloft, perhaps waiting for Finch to notice and replace it with a full one. "Otherwise, she must fancy herself Queen of the Coastline, and woe to any who cross her."

Sophia had already ordered the servants not to provide the Dowager Countess with more alcohol. She was glad to see their loyalty remained with her and didn't shift back to their former mistress on Teresa's reappearance. Fortunately, most of the footmen were unfamiliar with the Dowager Countess, but a few remained from her time, notably the butler, Finch.

"Mrs. Belmont had some good advice for me." Sophia didn't much care for Alva but the enemy of her enemy was her friend. "She's the one who suggested bringing guests to fill the Dower House and is responsible for bringing us such dear new acquaintances. Plus, what would I do without my Mr. Grant?" Warmly, she reached out to squeeze Louise Walden's hand, while flashing a smile in Grant's direction.

Gabriel, who had been leaning against the mantel and sipping his whiskey, stepped forward and clapped Mr. Grant on the back with a tad too much enthusiasm. Sophia wondered what had gotten into him. As a host, Gabriel had almost always been top-notch, but suddenly Sophia found his manners jarring.

"Grant, you're not drinking. Finch, fetch Mr. Grant a whiskey."

"No thank you, my lord. I never drink while on duty."

"Duty? This is dinner. Among friends! Walden has

a whiskey in his hand, as does Markham. Or do you prefer claret? Some men can't handle their whiskey."

Ah, Sophia saw what Gabriel was about then. The last time she'd seen him like this was just over a year ago with Lord Ralston. Her husband was jealous. Of Mr. Grant.

"I prefer not to drink," Grant said simply, holding his ground.

Sophia wished she could take Mr. Grant aside and tell him to let Finch bring him a watered-down whiskey to sip and placate Gabriel, but there was no opportunity.

Gabriel didn't say another word, but he exchanged a telling glance with Mr. Walden, who clearly enjoyed and could handle his whiskey. Lord Markham looked a little less sure of himself with a half-drained glass in his hand.

To Sophia's surprise, she heard Mr. Grant change his mind. "Very well, Mr. Finch. One whiskey, please. Straight up."

"There's a man for you," Walden said. "Didn't want to put your employer to shame, eh? I'll wager you could drink Lord Averford here under the table. No offense, Averford. We 'mericans stick together, and you Brits are too tea and toast to make a good show of proper drinking."

"No offense taken." Gabriel flashed the wide, predatory grin that Sophia remembered all too well. Her stomach tightened. The evening had taken a turn for the worse. "Proper drinking? Now keep in mind that we Brits invented proper. Didn't we, Markham? Speaking of wagers, perhaps we should play some billiards. If Markham and I beat you, you will give up the Dower House and remain here in the main house for the rest of your stay."

"Delightful!" Louise Walden jumped up and began to clap, then covered her mouth with her hands. "I'm sorry. It's just that I would like to stay in your beautiful house, Sophia. You've been so kind. But I suppose I shouldn't hope for my husband to lose."

Walden shook his head at his wife's show of enthusiasm. "And if we win?"

"Your stay is free of charge. I'll refund the money you paid to stay in the Dower House."

Sophia felt her anger rising. He would undo all her arrangements so easily? Not only that, but after a year away from her, he would run off to manly pursuits and leave her with his mother, who he'd never even mentioned was on the way? It was all she could do to hold her tongue, but she flashed him a glare. He was already looking at her, waiting for a reaction, his eyes filled with such tenderness that she suddenly realized he was doing it for her. To free up the Dower House so that he could move his mother back where she belonged, away from them. Even if it was only a short distance…

Walden nodded, agreeable until something suddenly seemed to occur to him. "But this fellow Grant works for you. How can I be certain he'll play fair and not throw it in your favor?"

"My honor and integrity, sir," Grant defended himself.

"You're fired, Grant." Gabriel turned his eyes from Sophia to Grant.

She wasn't sure if he was unable to face her reaction

or simply giving Grant his due. Under the circumstances, Grant deserved direct eye contact. But Gabriel had to know how sacking Grant was a slight to her and all the work she had done to maintain the estate in his absence. How could he? And so flippantly? Perhaps he'd never been thinking of her at all.

"If you win, you get your job back. I'm not a monster. There, Walden, you see? The man will be fighting for his position. You have an honest chance."

Sophia no longer knew what to think. If Gabriel won, his mother would be out of her way, at least most of the time, but Mr. Grant would be out of work. If Gabriel lost, he would be losing profit that Sophia had worked hard to gain. It seemed she would be the loser in any event. And when she finally got Gabriel all to herself, he was going to hear about it.

Six

It was well past midnight when the knock at her door roused her. She clicked on the light, reached for her silk wrapper, then changed her mind and left it. She knew Gabriel was knocking, and she had no intention of letting him in.

"Go away," she said through the door after crossing the room. "We can talk in the morning."

"It can't wait. Let me in."

"Trust me. You're better off waiting." The more she'd had a chance to toss and turn in the dark, thinking about his abandonment of her to go off and play billiards on a wager, the angrier she'd become.

"Sophia, please." His fingers scratched lightly at the wood, and she imagined he leaned his head against the door on the other side.

"Good night, Gabriel." She turned on her heel and started back to bed. The creak of the hinge made her look back to see Gabriel closing the door quietly behind him. "Gabriel! Get. Out."

"Not until you've heard what I have to say." He crossed the room, placed his hands on her shoulders, and locked his gaze on the rosy nipples standing to attention under her thin gown. "Uh."

She blushed and crossed her arms over her chest. "They're breasts, Gabriel. All women have them."

"But not all of them are so extraordinary," he mused, his eyes wide as he stared. "I imagine."

"You imagine other women's breasts?"

"No, I mean, I wouldn't know from looking at them anyway. I—" He ran his hand through his fair hair, ruffling it all out of place, then met her gaze. "God, Sophia, I've missed you. And your perfect breasts."

"You've been drinking, and now at last you've remembered that I live here too." Under her gown, she tapped her foot on the wood floor.

"I haven't had much to drink. Not really." He walked to the sitting area in the corner of her room and perched on an ottoman, tugging at his undone necktie. Perhaps his jacket lay abandoned in a corner of the billiard room. He wore only his white shirt, untucked, over his trousers. And the tie that he removed and tossed on one of her chairs. "And you've been on my mind all night. I've really made a mess of things."

She raised a brow. "I would say so."

"I wanted to be alone with you. Only you. So we could talk and work things out."

"You think a single conversation will fix all that we have wrong between us?"

"Of course not. Well, maybe. I could hope. But suddenly there were my mother and Lord Markham, and it all went downhill from there."

"You should have told me about your mother."

He arched a golden brow. "You might have mentioned inviting Charles."

She tipped her head. "I didn't invite him. Not exactly. He spoke of missing Yorkshire, and I said that he was welcome to visit. I hardly thought he would travel up immediately. At any rate, failing to mention an evening's candid conversation with Lord Markham is hardly as large an omission as you not telling me about the imminent arrival of your mother."

"Isn't it?" He stood. "You told him about us, Sophia. Personal things. And how was I to know that Mother's arrival was imminent? She was shopping in Paris. It usually takes her weeks."

She gasped. "Did Charles say as much? That I revealed personal details? Over billiards with a stranger in the room?"

Gabriel closed the distance between them and held two fingers in front of her nose. "Two. Two strangers. I don't know your Mr. Grant any better than I know Hugh Walden. Charles said that you confided in him. That's all. But he said it with the kind of sympathetic glance that made it seem to be coming from one divorced man to another, as if we now share some sort of unfortunate brotherhood."

"You're reading into it." She reached out to him, forgetting her intention to keep her distance. "It's not as bad as all that between us, certainly."

Had he ever considered divorce, if he believed her guilty of doing the same? Her stomach tensed, uneasy. She wished he would take her in his arms and hold her as tightly as he could and never let go. She couldn't just throw herself at him. Not without knowing how he felt.

He didn't reach for her. "I don't want to believe it is, but you were shooting daggers at me with your eyes. I was only trying to find a way to get my mother out of your house."

Her house. It sounded good to hear him say it. It was indeed her house, more than it had ever been before he'd run off. She'd made it truly her own, and she never meant to part with it again, at least not for long.

"Did you win?" She looked up at him, half hopeful, half afraid. She could write Grant a stellar recommendation and insist they fire Kenner too and take on the hiring of new people together. A new beginning.

"Of course not." He waved an arm. "I had to lose. As soon as I set the terms, I knew I had to lose. We've met the Waldens. We're friends now. It wouldn't be right to charge our friends money to visit us."

"No, you're right." She realized he had been thinking more clearly than she'd imagined all along. "I do like Louise. And Hugh. He's got a sense of humor. Once I met them, it felt odd to think of them paying to be our guests."

He smiled and reached for her again, running his palms over the thin silk of the sleeves of her nightdress. "There. We've made a decision together. It feels right, doesn't it? Working together instead of alone—or worse, against each other."

"What decision? You decided the outcome over billiards."

"Not really." He hazarded a step closer. "I did lose.

But we've agreed that it doesn't feel right to charge people to stay in the Dower House."

"It doesn't feel right to charge the Waldens." Allowing people to stay at the Dower House in exchange for money wasn't a bad plan in general. It had brought in some necessary income. She simply had to make it a point not to meet the people staying there.

"If we cancel the remaining reservations, we can send Mother back to where she belongs. Don't we both want to be rid of Mother?" He stepped even closer so that she could feel his warm length against her.

"Of course, but—"

He placed a finger to her lips. "Hush, love. I think we've done enough talking for the night."

Oh, so he was the one who got to decide when the conversation was over? Just like that? She shook her head. "No. I'm not done. I wouldn't feel right charging the Waldens, but Mr. Grant and I went to a lot of trouble to set up the rest of the reservations and—"

"Don't fret. He'll be here to cancel them all. I've given Mr. Grant his job back. I never really meant to take it away from him. I'll explain it all in depth to him tomorrow. But now, the night is for us."

Dazed, she looked up at him. He hadn't changed entirely, but there was a hint of the exotic about him now, perhaps a trace of sandalwood in his cologne. His eyes were heavy-lidded as he studied her face, focusing on her lips. His breathing slowed. A hand strayed from her arm to her breast, where he brushed a rose-tipped peak through her gown.

She felt an urgent tightening between her legs. "Gabriel, it's probably not a good idea to lose ourselves in—"

"So perfect," he said. "I've been waiting so long to be with you again. I don't think I can bear one more night apart from you. Please, Sophia. Let me sleep here with you."

"Sleep. Here?" she repeated, as if falling into a haze, drawn through his golden fringe of lashes to drown in his brown velvet gaze. Her whole body seemed to have come to life, blood thrumming, sweeping away from her brain to more sensitive areas…areas begging to be touched. His mouth met hers in slow, tender exploration.

She could barely control her own response to him, the overwhelming need. Her knees nearly buckled. Her hips swayed, arching toward his solidity. It was madness, this. Delicious, intoxicating madness. And for a moment, she'd been ready to let it take over.

The moment passed. Some little bit of sense that remained with her bubbled to the surface, breaking the spell. She placed a hand to his chest. "No. It's too soon. There's too much between us, too much that we need to work out."

"We will. But for now…" He stroked her cheek with the back of his hand, mouth hovering all too near.

His lower lip quivered, tempting her to kiss him again. But she would not surrender. She took his hands for no other reason than to keep them off her. One touch and she would be lost. "We can't expect physical gratification to obliterate all the problems between us."

He sighed, but hope still lit his eyes with a golden spark. "You enjoyed making love with me. Once."

She blushed. "I enjoyed it more than once. I enjoyed it every time, to be honest, but—"

"Then, why? Why push me away and pretend not to care for it? Why go to bed sobbing, alone, aching for love when I wanted so badly to give it to you? All those years, Sophia."

"You knew about the sobbing?"

"I could hear you. I'm right next door."

She tipped her head back and closed her eyes, unable to look at him while confessing. "Grief, certainly later on. Before that, following bad advice. I was a fool. I was young. I-I can't even imagine what I was thinking sometimes. But that's all behind us now, isn't it?" They had a whole new set of issues, or so it seemed. New obstacles to climb. Possibly insurmountable.

"I hope it is. I want us to have this." He brought her hand to his lips and kissed it. "But I can respect your wishes. I'll wait. Whatever it takes. We can undo all the damage we've done, and we can be stronger for it."

A delicate curl of heat smoldered from the glowing ember of hope within her, even as an icy snake of fear coiled in her belly ready to extinguish all possibilities. "What if it can't be undone, the damage? What if we find that we've never really been suited for each other?"

"Darling, how could you doubt it? Remember our first time?"

She nodded, her heart hammering against her rib cage. "Of course, but we've both changed so much. Everything has changed."

"And yet, so much remains the same. Let me show you." He did not wait for an answer but urged her up against the wall between the windows at the side of her bed, stretching her arms up over her head and pinning them there with one hand, while the other hand stroked the length of her body and his mouth claimed hers with a fiery intensity. His palm scorched her flesh through her gown, his fingers pausing at her navel before dipping lower to her mound, where they teased at her cleft.

Her breath caught in her throat, her approval trapped there with it. "Yes," she was about to cry. "Yes and yes and yes!" But he stopped abruptly, ending the kiss and drawing his hand from her. She shifted her hips, seeking his return.

Without a word, he began to back away, a wicked smile tugging at the corners of his lips. At the door, he paused. "Good night, sweet wife. And pleasant dreams."

❧

Gabriel's new motto, dreamed up as he walked away from Sophia, was "actions over words." Clearly, he had far greater success when he allowed his actions to do the talking for him. With words, she always managed to gain the upper hand. But with actions? She was powerless to resist him.

Actions spoke louder than words after all, didn't they? He couldn't remember who first said it, but he found himself in full agreement. Every argument he had to work his way into her bed could be met by a counterpoint, but that kiss? The kiss had her on the verge of saying yes. He could practically taste it on her tongue. But the risk was too great that she would regret it in the morning and all progress would be lost.

No, better to let her simmer, remembering the sensations that only he could give her, even if it was extraordinary torture for himself. In the throes of the raging need that gripped him, he would never be able to sleep without resorting to drastic measures. All too well, he had come to know the feel of his own hand. He wanted more. He wanted his wife's touch. Soon.

"Confidence," his father had always told him, "is the key to getting anything you want in life. A confident man always wins the day."

"A rich man wins the day," Marcus had always scoffed behind Father's back. "A man with full pockets and a title can afford to be confident." That was his younger brother, one to question everything he didn't read in books. Marcus had always possessed a natural ability to know how to act and what to say in most circumstances. Gabriel lacked such charm.

But he found that Father's advice worked to make up for what he lacked. No matter how self-conscious he'd felt at his core, he'd taken to putting on an air of superiority and carrying himself as if he hadn't a care in the world. He'd been the Baron of Travers, heir apparent to the Earl of Averford, too important to be overlooked. And now that he was the earl, pity to the man or woman who dared to cross him.

At least, that's the image he tried to project, and he succeeded at it most of the time. Only Sophia had the power to see through his ruse, if ever she bothered to look deep enough. So far, she hadn't looked much beneath his surface. But he refused to believe that they weren't suited. He simply had to try harder to bring them to a state of mutual understanding.

Contrary to her belief that her face or figure had first captured his attention, it was her confidence that had first held him rapt. Her resemblance to the Duchess of Marlborough might have drawn his gaze from across a crowded ballroom initially. When Alva Belmont was still Mrs. Vanderbilt, the notorious socialite had come to England scouting eligible noblemen to match with her daughter. Eager to score a triumph, Mother had tried to intrigue Gabriel with descriptions of the alluring American girl.

But Gabriel had no interest in marriage at the time, and even he could see that his title was not important enough to placate the demanding Alva. By all reports, only a prince or duke would do for the Vanderbilts. Still, Mother had considered it a cut when Alva Vanderbilt chose the Duke of Marlborough for her daughter without giving the future Earl of Averford any consideration. Even so, Mother had accepted any invitations to bring her into Alva's circle and had even issued a few of her own, most recently in Italy.

The idea of marriage hadn't tempted Gabriel until years later when Sophia's cornflower eyes met his from across that room. She didn't bat her lashes or look away like all of the other coquettes. She held his gaze and flashed him a dazzling smile before turning back to her friend. He'd realized at once that she wasn't the celebrated duchess, as he had supposed, but a much more fascinating debutante.

His breath had caught as they'd made that brief

connection, and he'd needed more than a moment to recover. In that instant, he recognized her as his own, his soul's match. The confidence she exuded made it immediately clear to him that of all women, only she possessed the proper bearing to elicit sighs of admiration when standing by his side. He had to have her. No one else would do.

Her confidence had allowed Sophia to remain undaunted, head held high under his mother's early interrogations and later attempts to bully her. Anyone who could stand up to his mother and escape apparently unscathed earned his undying admiration.

Unfortunately, that same confidence had led him to believe, perhaps erroneously, that Sophia had never really needed him. And how he yearned to be needed! If only she'd been able to ask for what she wanted from him. But she would never allow herself to appear vulnerable. In any event, he would never take advantage of her. Though perhaps he had taken her for granted, refused to see any signs that she struggled on her own without asking anything of him. And along came Lord Ralston at the ready...

Too late to change the past. They could only move forward, both of them with eyes open, ready to see what they had in each other and how it was worth every effort to keep.

Seven

AFTER GABRIEL'S VISIT, SLEEP HAD PROVEN IMPOSSIBLE. Sophia thought about giving up, just going to his room and crawling into bed with him. But she had no idea what time the valet would come to wake him, and word would get around the house fast. Not that it was any better to keep the servants aware that the earl and countess didn't share a room, and waking up with her own husband would hardly create a scandal. Why did she even care what anyone thought? It was her life. Let them talk.

Deep down, she knew it was more than what anyone whispered behind her back that kept her from seeking out Gabriel. It was her damnable pride. She couldn't bear to let him think she was vulnerable, not when she'd gone to such effort to create an impression of strength. And she *was* strong! She was fierce. She looked in her mirror every morning and told herself so. Just let anyone try to challenge her. Now that the Dowager Countess had returned, Sophia needed to reassure herself more than ever. The woman sent shivers up her spine.

Of course, Sophia had never let Gabriel's mother see her show any hint of fear, and she refused to do so now just because she'd had no warning of the woman's arrival. Sophia had no doubt that Gabriel's mother had deliberately given him the false impression that she would be away much longer just so that she could gain an upper hand with the element of surprise. Sophia smiled, imagining how that surprise had backfired once Teresa showed up at the Dower House to find it occupied.

Sophia was out of bed pacing her floor when the door opened. Instead of Jenks, as she'd expected, she turned to find Jane, their newest maid. Unsatisfied with the girl's references, Mrs. Hoyle had recommended against hiring her, but Sophia had taken a liking to fair Jane and had decided to give her a chance.

"I'm sorry, Lady Averford. I hope I'm not intruding. Mrs. Jenks has been held up and asked me to bring yer clean linens." The maid closed the door behind her and headed straight to the closet with her laundry basket.

"It's good to see you, Jane. I've been meaning to ask how you're getting on here at Thornbrook Park." She'd worried about Mrs. Hoyle making things hard on the newcomer out of some misguided sense of revenge on Sophia for going against her advice, but even Hoyle had had to admit she was wrong about the girl. Jane was a hard worker, Hoyle had confessed to Sophia, and she was catching on quickly.

"I like it here, Lady Averford. Thank ye for asking. Plenty o' work to keep me busy, and everyone has been so nice."

"I'm glad to hear it." Sophia smiled. "Keep up the good work."

"Is there anything I can do for ye until Mrs. Jenks arrives?" Jane asked eagerly. "I can run yer bath or arrange yer toilette."

"Thank you, Jane."

By the time Jenks came in, she found Sophia nearly ready. Jane took her leave and allowed Jenks to continue, but Sophia only needed her maid to do up the last few buttons at the back of her dress, a rose-colored chiffon over silk with just a flutter of lace at the shoulders for sleeves.

"And the pearls, my lady?" Jenks asked as Sophia started for the door. "You usually wear your long strand with that dress."

"Not the pearls." She returned to her toilette. "The aquamarine on the long platinum chain, the one set with tiny diamonds and an amethyst."

"An unusual choice for your dress, my lady."

"Yes, it is." Sophia held still while Jenks fastened it. "But it's the right one. Thank you, Jenks. That will be all."

Sophia headed for the stairs. The aquamarine had been a gift from Gabriel on their honeymoon, when they were both so full of hope and joy. He'd draped it over her pillow and waited for her to find it when they went to bed at night. She couldn't miss it, of course. The central aquamarine was enormous and caught the light just so.

It had delighted her, but Gabriel had been all apologies. He'd been trying to find a stone to match her eyes, he'd said. The aquamarine was a disappointment, far too light. He should have gone with a sapphire. Nonsense, she'd told him. Nothing could make her happier than the one he'd chosen for her. She hoped he would remember when he saw her wearing it.

The breakfast room was empty with the exception of a footman standing by the sideboard.

"The earl hasn't come down?" she asked.

"He has, my lady. He's in his office now. Would you like some tea?"

"His office?" A day ago, it had been her office. She hoped it would be *their* office. Why hadn't he waited for her? "Thank you, nothing for me." She had lost her appetite.

Outside the office door, she paused to listen to the voices. Mr. Grant was with Gabriel, as evidenced by the baritone questioning. She didn't hear Cornelius Kenner's high-pitched, nearly childish voice. Deciding against knocking, she went on in.

"Starting without me?"

Both men stood on sight of her. "Without you? I didn't think you would have an interest in our exchange of figures and speculations. In fact, I thought you would still be in bed."

Mr. Grant had the good sense to blush at such a suggestion. As far as Grant knew, Sophia rose with the dawn each morning.

"Still in bed when there's business to be done? Highly unlikely." She tipped back her head and laughed as if they were all having a great joke. It was better than seething inside. Gabriel really didn't seem to understand that she did not intend to stop being part of Thornbrook Park's daily planning. She did not take the chair next to Grant but went around to her husband's side of the desk. "A little cramped back here for both of us. I suppose we could take out that table and bookshelf and add a second desk."

"You have a salon for your writing and letters." Gabriel remained ignorant, or he did a good job of pretending to be.

"My salon? Of course, yes. But that's not a proper place of business. I need to be here with the records and ledgers. We've been meeting here every morning for just about a year now. Haven't we, Mr. Grant? I don't see why anything needs to change."

"Because I've returned, darling." Gabriel kissed her forehead dismissively before sweeping her aside to take his chair. "Grant and I have a great many things to discuss, most notably his change of title."

For lack of a chair, she perched her bottom on the edge of the desk, perilously close to Gabriel's writing arm. She leaned at an angle, twisting at the waist and balancing on her arm to enable her to face both Gabriel and Grant.

Gabriel flashed her a look that seemed to ask if she honestly intended to stay put. Indeed she did. She hiked her skirt up a few inches to draw his attention to her stocking-clad ankles and twisted her necklace with her one free hand. Why did he not seem to notice the aquamarine?

"Now where's Mr. Kenner? We can't get started without him, can we?" she asked, assuming command. She feared the answer might be that Kenner had been fired, though perhaps it would be for the best.

"I sent Kenner off to answer some mail. Once I told

him what to say, of course. That's his job, after all, as my secretary."

"Your secretary?" She felt her brow shoot up sharp as a dagger. "Don't you mean *our* secretary?"

Gabriel looked at her through narrowed eyes as if he couldn't quite figure out what kind of game she was playing or how far she meant to go with it. Anger burned in her chest. He had better start to realize that she wasn't playing at all.

"No, darling," he said quite calmly, as an adult might humor a child. "He's my secretary. If you want one, you're going to have to run off and get your own."

"Get my own secretary?" She shot Grant a look. "I thought I had one."

"An overpaid one, if you mean Grant. He has claimed his proper title at last. Lady Averford, meet our new estate agent, Mr. Wesley Grant."

Grant played along, tipping his head in her direction. So easily he had defected. And Kenner too. Oh, they were maddening, the lot of them! She slipped to her feet and faced her husband. To hell with Grant.

"Do you really mean to cut me out of Thornbrook Park's business affairs, after everything I've done? I assure you that I won't take kindly to it." She crossed her arms and awaited his response. He'd asked her if they were enemies, and she'd said no, but he was doing a darn fine imitation of one.

"You've done a wonderful job, Sophia." He reached for her hands, unfolding them from her arms and bringing them to his lips, where he gently kissed each one at the center knuckle. "You really rose to the occasion in my absence, and I'm grateful. Thornbrook Park owes much of its success in the past year to you."

"Much?" She froze in place, but mentally prepared to pull back her hands and contemplate putting her knuckles to better use.

"Some credit goes to Grant and to Mr. Kenner, of course, as well."

"Which reminds me... Kenner's salary." She would stay as focused as she could, given the circumstances. "Have we amended it? If I was overpaying Mr. Grant for the office, certainly we're paying Kenner too much to be a mere secretary."

"Absolutely." Gabriel nodded. "He has already agreed to a reduced salary. Hasn't he, Grant?"

"In keeping with the expectation of a secretary's wages, yes. He was far more agreeable than I expected him to be." Which was to say, in Grant's way of expressing himself, that it was far more of a reduction than he would have accepted in the same position. Sophia knew the man well. And yet, not well enough to have guessed how easily he would take orders from Gabriel instead of waiting for Sophia's approval.

"A good man, Kenner. I'll need to see the report of his new wages so I know what to pay my secretary, in keeping with fairness."

Gabriel laughed. "Your secretary? I expect you can put out an inquiry to a secretarial school and get a good girl for less than half what I'm paying Kenner."

"A good girl?" She looked at Gabriel as if she'd never seen him before in her life. Who was this man, and what had he done with her husband? Oh, but of course. He was acting exactly as he always had, as she would expect. It was she who had changed. And perhaps *only* she who had changed, despite his earlier protests. Cook her dinner? She doubted he could boil water. "Why isn't a good girl worth as much as your boy Kenner?"

Gabriel spread out his hands as if frustrated with having to keep explaining to her. "It's just the way it is, dearest. You know how the world works."

She harrumphed. Out loud. She believed it to be her first actual harrumph, and it felt good. "For now. I know how it works for now. But one day soon, you'll wake up and find that things have changed all around. Women will stop allowing themselves to be taken for granted, and where will you men be then?" She headed for the door, through with his patronizing and refusing to make it into more of an argument with Grant watching.

She paused at the door and turned back. Gabriel stood, gape-mouthed, seemingly at a loss for words. "Alone, that's where. You'll be sleeping in your beds alone wondering where it all went wrong, while women are up and about ruling the world. Mark my words, Gabriel Thorne…" She shook a finger in his direction for effect.

"I'm sorry." He shook his fair leonine head as if distracted. "I've been too busy marking your necklace. The aquamarine! You're wearing it again."

"I—yes." She followed his gaze to her chest. How she'd hoped that he would notice and be touched, but not when she was so desperately struggling to make the point about equality for women! "Yes, I am. But the point is…"

He came around the desk and closed the distance, taking her in his arms. "You do believe there's hope for us after all."

The idiot! He practically beamed at her like a love-sick schoolboy. All she wanted was for him to take her seriously, but yet…how could she resist him when he looked at her like that?

"You know I do. But right now, I'm frustrated with you for not hearing me out properly."

"I'm sorry, darling. You were saying?" He cocked a golden brow and waited for her to finish, all the while gripping her hands and swinging her arms between them like children about to skip off and play hopscotch.

"I was saying that I need to be involved in the business affairs."

"No, that wasn't it." He shook his head and looked back to Grant for confirmation. "She'd moved on, hadn't she? Something about women being worth as much as men in a secretarial capacity? But I don't think so, if you look at the facts. I do believe women are a far more affordable resource."

"A resource?" She felt the heat rushing to her face.

"So go ahead and hire your secretary." He kissed her red, hot cheek. "I don't mind. We'll go over the salary requirements later. I can have Kenner draft a letter if you like. But for now, perhaps you should go eat some breakfast. You look like you could use some tea, maybe a nice poached egg."

"An egg?" She threw up her hands, exasperated. How could he be so obtuse? She was certain he was doing it deliberately, playing ignorant to keep her from demanding her place at his side perhaps? Or maybe he was that stupid and she'd been so smitten that she'd never noticed, a definite possibility. "Yes, exactly what I need. Why didn't I think of it? I'm going to have some eggs."

"All right. I'll see you later." Gabriel had already turned to head back to his desk. "Just close the door on your way out. Thank you."

She closed the door with so much force she thought she might rip it from the frame, and she stormed off down the hall. She needed a secretary immediately, someone of her own choosing and not one that Gabriel found for her with the help of the traitorous Mr. Grant or Mr. Kenner. She knew exactly where she could find one. She rang for Mr. Finch to fetch her hat and gloves, and demanded that he have Mr. Dale pull the car around.

❧

Gabriel resumed his position at the desk. "Thank you, Mr. Grant. You played your role to perfection."

"Fortunately, I didn't have to say much. I dread the idea of the countess believing that I've crossed her. She's a formidable force."

Gabriel waved a hand dismissively. "She's too angry at me to direct any venom your way, but it was a necessary deception. If she knew I was working against her just to get my mother out of her way, she would dig her heels in harder. I knew she was headstrong, but I've never seen her quite like this, so…charged up."

He paused for a minute to consider the fire that had glowed white-hot in Sophia's cornflower eyes.

Strangely, it hadn't put him off but had made him all the more eager to get her alone. Had Grant not been in the room, Gabriel might have pressed Sophia up against the door and tried to kiss her again. Her determination was oddly seductive.

"Are you sure it's necessary to cancel all of the reservations, my lord? Think of the income to the estate."

"It's necessary. I know that you and Sophia worked hard on your plans to transform the Dower House into guest accommodations, but—well, if you think my wife is a formidable force, you should spend more time with my mother. The two of them in one house for more than another week could bring on the apocalypse. They're both on their best behavior now, determined to be civil and polite, but just you wait. It won't take much. One perceived slight on either side, and all hell breaks loose."

"And there you are caught in the middle. Awkward to have to side with one or the other."

"With Sophia, of course. I'm always on the side of my wife."

"As any smart man would be. Your mother must expect as much." Grant shrugged. Clearly he had no idea what Gabriel was up against. Then again, he had worked for Alva Belmont. "The countess isn't going to forgive you all that easily if you change her plans."

"I'm only keeping her at bay for now. Once we've settled the matter of canceling future reservations, I will seek her out with an apology for my behavior and present her with a gift." He hoped the offer of a gift could make up for his horrible behavior and keep the peace between them.

"Jewelry?" Grant stroked his chin, considering.

Gabriel shook his head. "I always give her jewelry. It no longer makes much of an impact." Though she had shown up wearing his aquamarine. Certainly it was a sign that she was eager to make up with him. "Perhaps an investment. Something to show her that I admire her business sense."

Grant nodded. "Stock?"

"Land." It had to be land. What did he value more than Thornbrook Park, after all? It was the only way to show Sophia that he loved her more than he loved even his ancestral estate. And by gifting her with a parcel of the land, to be all her own and not shared with him, he would be showing her that he trusted her judgment above all. It was perfect. "Some bit of reassurance that no matter what happens, she will always have a part of Thornbrook Park of her very own, to use as she chooses without any input from me."

"But which parcel?"

"On the western border, there are a few acres of fairly flat land with a brook running through it all." His favorite spot for fishing. He'd brought Sophia there for a picnic and she'd lost her temper with him because he'd paid more attention to his rod than to her. By putting that land in her hands, he would show her that his love for her exceeded all else. "She could build a cottage there or a little pavilion. Whatever her heart desires."

"Are you sure? What if she decides to sell?"

She wouldn't sell. He felt fairly certain that she'd become as attached to the land as he was. "It would be her choice, and I suppose I would have to be the one to buy it back. Draw up the papers with Kenner. I want to present it to her as soon as possible."

"As you wish, Lord Averford."

"Good. Now tell me, Grant, how soon can we have my mother back at the Dower House where she belongs?" However quickly, Gabriel was certain it could not be soon enough.

Eight

"To Tilly Meadow Farm, Mr. Dale," Sophia informed the chauffeur once she was settled in the stiff leather seat.

"Right away, my lady." He adjusted the rearview mirror and met her gaze before turning his eyes to the road.

They arrived in no time at all since the tenant farm was just a few miles from Thornbrook Park. Sophia put on her imperious face and waited for Dale to open the door for her. Normally, her visits to the farm were warm and friendly social calls. Today, she needed to take a more authoritative position. She couldn't risk Prudence Cooper turning down her request.

"I've warned you about showing up here in your fine clothes." Mrs. Dennehy was as straightforward as always when she greeted Sophia at the door. "We like to put visitors to work no matter what they're wearing."

Sophia smiled. "What would you have me do? I'm up for a challenge."

Leave it to Mrs. Dennehy to bring Sophia's guard

down immediately. The silver hair and slight build might fool some people into underestimating her on sight, but the old woman proved to be a commanding force as soon as she opened her mouth.

Mrs. Dennehy's eyes widened. "You're a brave soul, Lady Averford. Unfortunately, no rough work today. The cows have already been milked. You can help me shell peas while we talk."

"Shelling peas it will be. But I'm here to speak to Prudence Cooper. Is she available?"

Mrs. Dennehy nodded. "Who do you think has assigned me the task of shelling peas? She's in the kitchen. We can sit with her in there."

They found Prudence rolling out dough for a pie on the enormous wood-block countertop. At the sight of Sophia, she set aside her rolling pin and wiped her hands on her apron. "I'm sorry. I wasn't aware we had a visitor. I must look a fright."

"You're lovely as usual," Sophia said, and she meant it. Even with flour dusting her brown hair, sweet-faced Prudence looked like an angel from a Christmas card. "I understand we're shelling peas?"

The peas sat divided between a colander and a porcelain bowl on the table in the corner, with another empty bowl to one side. Sophia didn't wait for an invitation to take her seat near one of the bowls. She stripped off her gloves and set them in her lap.

"Goodness, no. Let's go to the parlor. I'll make some tea." Prudence shot Mrs. Dennehy a look as if to say, "How could you expect the countess to shell peas?"

Mrs. Dennehy shrugged without remorse and

took the seat opposite Sophia. She judged people by their character, not by titles. Sophia respected her immensely.

"I like it in here. The kitchen is so bright and cheerful. I've always liked gingham curtains. Did you make them, Mrs. Cooper?" When she was younger, Sophia had been skilled at embroidery, but she hadn't had an occasion to pick up a needle and thread for years.

"I did. Years ago now, when we first arrived." The Coopers had lived at Tilly Meadow Farm since Gabriel's brother had returned from his self-imposed exile to Thornbrook Park three years ago. Prudence Cooper was the widow of Marcus's best friend who'd died at war, and Marcus had worked out a plan to get Prudence and her children out of London to help Mrs. Dennehy on the farm in the fresh country air.

For Sophia, stitching had been an accomplishment, something to show off to tempt a husband, that she'd had the luxury to abandon after marriage. For Prudence Cooper, sewing was a necessary skill to stretch resources in a household with a limited budget. How different life had been for the two of them, Sophia and Prudence, two women of about the same age from such different backgrounds. Sophia felt more humble and less haughty by the minute. Perhaps she just didn't have it in her to appear above it all any longer. Who was the better woman? Someone who had been born with every privilege, or someone who worked so hard for everything she had?

"I guess it has been some years since I've been in this kitchen." In the past, she had been able to put on airs. She was the countess. Suddenly, she couldn't imagine how she could even pretend to be more important than Prudence or Mrs. Dennehy. "By all means, please finish your pie, Mrs. Cooper. We can talk more seriously once it's in the oven baking. I must confess that I've never shelled peas. How is it done?"

"Ha, and why would you? You probably have a footman hired just for the purpose of shelling peas." Mrs. Dennehy laughed, but not at Sophia's expense.

Sophia laughed along. "That sort of task falls to a kitchen maid."

"I see." Mrs. Dennehy demonstrated as they spoke, pinching off the stem end of the pod, pulling a stringy fiber to open the seam, and using her thumb to spill the peas into a bowl. She put the empty shell in another bowl. "In that case, the poor girl probably has other jobs too, like scrubbing pots and pans. Women are always expected to work harder than men."

Sophia couldn't argue that, though she knew both men and women worked very hard at Thornbrook Park. "She has other jobs, mostly to help our cook, Mrs. Mallows, as needed. But the scullery maid is the one who scrubs pots."

"Imagine, Prudence? A maid just to scrub pots!" Mrs. Dennehy rolled her eyes.

"It does seem indulgent, but I'm grateful for the help. Especially when we're entertaining a crowd." Sophia picked up a pea and made her first attempt. "Oh, they zip right open, don't they? What do you do with the shells?"

"Put them in soups and stews for flavor. Sometimes we save them for the pigs."

"The pigs, yes. I'd forgotten that you've added some pigs recently."

"They're great fun for the boys," Prudence said. "Though I'm afraid young Finn might be getting too attached, and there goes any hope for bacon."

"He'll learn." Mrs. Dennehy nodded. "They all do."

Brandon, Prudence's oldest boy, was nearly eighteen and doing a man's work around the farm, but the youngest, Finn, was still only ten years old. "And the girls? Do they help with the livestock?"

"They spoil me." Mrs. Dennehy smiled with pride. In the short time that they'd all lived together, she had become like a grandmother to the Cooper children. "Mostly, they work around the house. I don't think I've made a bed since they've moved in. If they had their way, they would have me sit my sorry old bones in a rocking chair day in and out. But to work is to live! I have to keep moving. They also help me with the milking. Emily, especially, has an interest in making cheese."

"And Anna?" Sophia asked reluctantly, afraid to hear something to put her off the mission that had brought her to the farm. "Has she come to like life on the farm? I recall that she was initially the most reluctant of your four to leave London."

"She was," Prudence agreed. "She has come to think of it as home here, but she's still a dreamer. There's just not much society for a young girl on a farm."

Sophia nodded. "It's Anna I've come to discuss. She's sixteen now, old enough to seek out some new opportunities. I'm sure you dread to part with her, but I was wondering if I could ask her to come live at Thornbrook Park and act as my secretary."

"Your secretary?" Prudence sounded shocked. "But she doesn't have any training."

"A minor issue, I believe. I can teach her what I want from her, and she can learn more from Mr. Kenner." Keeping Mr. Kenner too busy to see to any of Gabriel's requests. It was the perfect plan.

"Your estate manager?"

"My husband's secretary, actually. Mr. Grant is now acting as our estate manager. It would be a wonderful opportunity for Anna to pick up some new skills, not to mention the social advantages. At Thornbrook Park, she would be able to meet more people and—"

"Expand her circle to include more of the right people?" Mrs. Dennehy arched a thin silver brow.

"More worldly people, perhaps," Sophia acknowledged. "I certainly wouldn't say they were all the right people, but I would do my best to watch over her, knowing that she is still young and impressionable."

"I trust you, Lady Averford. I know you would be a good influence on her. And she wouldn't be so very far away after all."

"You're welcome to call on her any time, and I'm sure she'll come back here when she feels lonely or homesick or desperate for a slice of your delicious pie. It smells so good and you just put it in the oven."

"Strawberry rhubarb. I would be happy to send it over to the house for you when it's cooled."

"Not necessary, but thank you. I wouldn't want to surprise Mrs. Mallows with an unplanned addition to the menu."

"Of course. Brandon will be glad to hear it. Strawberry rhubarb is his favorite, and I believe he's counting on this one to be his snack later today once he returns from harvesting."

"Brandon has done well on the farm. Marcus predicted he would thrive here."

"All of us have. We're grateful to Mrs. Dennehy for taking us on."

"Where would I be without you and the children, Prudence dear? You've given this old woman new joy, and some much-needed relief. I would never have admitted it earlier, but it was getting difficult to keep up with everything on my own out here."

"If you can't spare Anna, I understand," Sophia said, though she was hoping to return home triumphant with her own secretary at her side. "But you should know that I plan to pay her well, a salary befitting a personal secretary to a countess."

"Let's see what she has to say about all this, shall we?" Prudence suggested. "I can spare her if she would like to go."

"Then we'll talk wages." Mrs. Dennehy nodded. "I'm prepared to negotiate on her behalf, Lady Averford. Keep that in mind."

"I'm sure you wouldn't let her go for any less than you feel she's worth."

⇛

Hours later, Sophia returned triumphant, an eager Anna at her side.

"Have the footmen see to her things, Mr. Finch. Anna Cooper has become part of the household. My secretary." Sophia, on tiptoes, looked over and around the butler, eager to see if Gabriel was walking about the hall. No sign of him.

Anna, wide-eyed, spun a circle at the center of the room. "Your house is grand, Lady Averford. Very grand. I'm to live here, truly?"

"Truly. I find it easier not to have to send a driver for my secretary when I need her." She said the word "secretary" much louder than necessary, hoping to be overheard.

"Of course." Anna blushed quite prettily. Sophia had only just noticed how Anna had grown into her looks. As a child, she'd had squinty eyes and pinched cheeks, giving her the appearance of a shrew in the making. But with age, her face had filled out, as cherubic as her mother's, and her doe-like eyes looked all around the room, apparently taking in every detail.

"Put her in the yellow room, Finch." Sophia stripped off her gloves and handed them to the butler.

"Oh." Anna looked confused. "Mother said a lady keeps her gloves on, even to take tea."

Sophia smiled. "Perhaps in more formal situations, and certainly at dinner. Normally, though, I prefer to be without them. Since it's just us, we can do as we like." In the past, Sophia had been more of a slave to convention, but she'd learned to live as she preferred in her own house when they weren't keeping company. She refused to allow the fact that her mother-in-law was in residence to change her daily routine.

Anna smiled and began tugging her gloves off one finger at a time. "I do like yellow. So lively. A room of my own!"

Sophia didn't have the heart to tell her that nothing in the room was actually yellow any longer. They'd simply been calling it the yellow room for as long as she could recall. It didn't seem to matter. She wasn't sure the girl had heard much of anything she'd said after promising her that she would have her own room. She couldn't even be sure that Anna understood she would be receiving wages for her work, despite Mrs. Dennehy's bargaining on her behalf.

"You've always shared with your sister?"

Anna nodded absently, clearly taken with the arrangement of flowers in the painted vase on the sideboard. "Always."

"You might find it lonely here at first, but you seem the sort to make friends quickly. Feel free to invite your sister to stay a night or two. Mr. Finch can arrange for our driver to fetch Emily any time you choose to invite her."

"I expect I'll be too busy for visitors. When do we get started? Have you any letters to write? I've got neat handwriting, very precise, or so Mother often says."

Sophia shook her head. "No letters today. But since you're so eager, we can introduce you around. Mr. Finch, where's the earl hiding? Is he in his study?"

"No, my lady. He went out some time ago."

"Out?" She cocked a brow. Hunting, no doubt. He probably couldn't wait to get his hands on his rifle again. "Mr. Kenner, then? Or Mr. Grant?"

Sophia meant to have words with both men regarding their treachery, but she especially had Mr. Grant in her crosshairs after his little show of support for her husband that morning. She wouldn't stand for the servants taking sides…unless they were all on hers.

"Mr. Grant is in the office. I'll send Mr. Kenner along shortly."

"As soon as you manage to locate him, you mean to say? Check the terrace. I think you might find him there." She appreciated that Finch, ever the diplomat, had simply referred to the workspace as "the office" without assigning possession of it to either earl or countess. Well played. "Come along, Anna. Meet Mr. Grant."

Anna stayed on Sophia's heels as she walked off down the hall. In time, perhaps, the girl would gain some confidence. Sophia did not bother to knock once she reached the office but breezed on in. Mr. Grant looked up with some surprise and shuffled the papers he'd been reading around on the desk before getting to his feet.

"Good day, Lady Averford. What can I do for you?"

"What can you do for me? That seems a great improvement from this morning when you were all eager to please my husband at my expense."

He shook his head. "It wasn't like that. My apologies. I—"

She held up a hand to stop him. "No need for excuses, Grant. My husband can be a very demanding man. It's good that you've let him believe you do his bidding. It will suit me to keep him complacent."

Grant's mouth quirked up in the corner, just a hint, a sure sign that he was no longer on sure footing around her. *Good. Let him be unsettled.*

After a quick knock, Mr. Kenner entered without awaiting an answer. "You called for me?"

"Yes, Mr. Kenner. Now that I have you both here, allow me to present Anna Cooper. Anna is my new secretary." She crossed her arms over her chest. "Mr. Kenner, I'll expect you to take her under your wing. She might be young, but she's eager and completely devoted. Come to think of it, you two might learn some things from her."

Kenner remained all business, nodding in her direction. Mr. Grant grimaced slightly in response to Sophia's pointed words, but he recovered in time to flash a charming smile in Anna's direction. "Lovely to meet you, Miss Cooper."

"You may call me Anna." The blush again, paired with downcast eyes. Sophia realized she would have to keep a close eye on the girl. Her disarming innocence could make her a great favorite among the menservants.

"In which case, I expect you to call me Wesley."

Kenner fidgeted and pushed his spectacles up on his nose. "Cornelius."

"Mr. Kenner, why don't you take Anna on a brief tour of the house. Show her the writing desk in my parlor, where I expect we'll take care of our more informal correspondence. At least, until we move a second desk in here."

"Miss Cooper." Kenner, a slave to formality, held his arm out for Anna to take and led her off, leaving Sophia alone with Mr. Grant.

"Now that leaves us to conduct our business. Perfect."

"At your service, Lady Averford. As always."

"I'm glad to hear it. So tell me, what important matters did you and my husband discuss without me this morning?"

After a moment's hesitation, he held his hands up, palms to the air. "Not much, really. There was the business of my promotion."

"To your proper title at last." She walked around the desk and took her seat, gesturing to Mr. Grant that he should sit as well. With Gabriel out-of-doors, now was her chance. She didn't mean to be quick with Grant. "The one I always meant for you to have. But surely, there was more than that."

"Mr. Kenner's position clarified, of course."

"Of course. And?"

He kept his gaze down, as if suddenly fascinated by the pattern on the carpet. "This and that, going over accounts."

"I realize it's awkward for you to be between us just now, Mr. Grant, while you believe my husband and I are working against each other. Let me assure you that it's not the case."

"It's not?" he blurted out before she supposed he could stop himself, his gaze darting to hers.

"No." She folded her hands on the desk. "We both want what's in the best interest of Thornbrook Park. You know my way of working, and I suppose you'll get to know his. I don't know his as well as I could, I confess, having allowed myself to be kept in the dark for so many years. But it's a new day. The sun is shining. And I can guess what the earl might have in mind."

Mr. Grant gave himself away with the slow upturn

at the corner of his lips. He didn't think she could guess the half of it, and perhaps he was right. But she wasn't entirely naive, not anymore. "He has instructed you to cancel the guesthouse reservations, has he not?"

A flinch. Yes, she was on to something. Grant cleared his throat. "We discussed so many things."

"And yet you said, 'Not much, really,' when I asked you."

"I suppose I did. I'm useless without my notes, as you know."

"I know no such thing. Don't be reluctant with me, Grant. We've been friends for so long now. I need to know that I can rely on you. As a friend, if nothing more."

His pride wounded by the suggestion that he hadn't done his best at something, he looked up. "You can rely on me, Lady Averford. Please don't doubt me."

"I won't. As long as you do your best not to cancel those reservations. At least, not in any hurry. You can cancel the next few, if you must, to alleviate my husband's concerns. I realize that he wants to move his mother back to the Dower House, and I know he's doing it for me. He simply doesn't understand how my tolerance has grown. I'm much stronger than he knows."

"He thinks very highly of you."

"I should hope so. I am his wife. And I can certainly stand for his mother to be under our roof, at least for a little while. Until she gets bored here. She's used to Italy and society. I don't think she'll last long at Thornbrook Park, even in the Dower House. We're simply too dull for the worldly Dowager Countess." At least, she

planned to be. She would take a sudden loathing to
entertainments of all kinds. No large dinners or grand
affairs. "And by the time she leaves, Gabriel might realize how the income from running a guesthouse boosts
our finances enough to make a difference."

Mr. Grant nodded along. "It does bring in a
tidy sum."

"I knew you would agree with me. You helped me
to see the sense of it in the first place, my dear man."

Grant blushed. Flattery could get her everywhere.
"This could work," he said. "I'll cancel these next
two, and we'll see what to do from there. No need for
Lord Averford to be concerned."

"No need at all. He doesn't even need to know
that you haven't canceled them all. You might, in due
time, but why rush into things?"

"Why indeed," Grant agreed.

"It's all I ask. Let's just give the earl some time to
get accustomed to being at home, and then see how
things can change." She got to her feet. "I'll leave
you now. No sense looking like conspirators caught
hatching a plan. Perhaps you can catch up to Anna
and Mr. Kenner. Make sure he's teaching her all the
right things. And then you can give the girl some time
on her own to get settled. We don't want her to be
overwhelmed on her first day."

"Right away, Lady Averford." He reached across
and snatched up the papers he'd been studying when
she'd walked in on him, the stack she'd planned to go
through to see what else Gabriel had put before him.
"Until later."

Before she could stop him, he turned on his heel

and fled, increasing her suspicion that Gabriel was up to something. Something Grant continued to hide from her despite their warm little talk. She would find out. They could count on it. More the pity for them if they underestimated her.

Nine

AFTER SETTLING HIS BUSINESS OF THE MORNING WITH Grant and Kenner, Gabriel decided on a walk about the grounds. He still hadn't looked it all over since coming home, and he'd been eager to see what had changed, and what had remained quite happily the same. By late in the afternoon, he'd made it all around the main yard, with stops in the garden to pick out some flowers to be sent in to adorn Sophia's dressing table and a prolonged visit to the kennels, where he enlisted Chauncey, one of the younger fox terriers, to accompany him for the remainder of his amble. He hadn't planned on stopping at his son's grave, but somehow he ended up there. His feet just led that way before his mind caught up to where he was headed.

"Edward." He addressed the stone, though he hadn't expected anyone could hear him. "And Father. I hope you're looking after our boy."

They had buried the baby next to the earl, some distance from the chapel yard on a small stretch of green surrounded by wildflowers at the edge of the

wood. The flowers had recently been cut back, necessary from time to time to keep them from taking
over. Gabriel made it a point to only visit once a year,
in the springtime, when he normally left a colorful
kite. He hadn't made it this year yet, and he hadn't
been planning to stop. He'd come without a kite. He
supposed he would make two visits to make up for
missing the last.

He had no idea what happened to the kites after he
left them. He liked to think that the wind, or perhaps
neighborhood children, carried them off. More likely,
it was the groundskeeper. Perhaps a corner of the shed
was filled with old kites that had never been flown,
representing all those years he hadn't been able to
spend with his son.

"Next time, I'll bring your kite, Edward. I promise." And before he knew what had come over him,
the Earl of Averford dissolved into tears. Big, heaving
sobs. He dropped to his knees with the weight of the
grief on his soul.

The dog had been running around chasing a squirrel across the grass, but suddenly he was at Gabriel's
side, as if sensing his emotional distress. Chauncey
jumped up and sniffed at Gabriel's shoulder, then
hopped onto the earl's knees and began licking his
face. After a minute, Gabriel found his tears had turned
to laughter. He rubbed the dog between the ears. "All
right, Chauncey. Down, boy."

Perhaps he would reward the dog with a stay at the
house. There was nothing like a dog to bring joy and
lighten the mood. Plus, he could use the companionship should Sophia decide to stop speaking to him.

"Gabriel." He startled at the sound of her voice behind him. Had she seen him crying?

"Sophia." He stood and turned to find her looking as breathtaking as ever, even in her simple cotton frock. She'd changed clothes since morning, no more aquamarine. He hoped it wasn't intended as a slight.

She carried a bouquet of forget-me-nots, indicating that her visit had been planned and not just a chance wandering. She always left forget-me-nots. He'd never accompanied her, not since that first visit when he'd showed her where he'd laid their son to rest while she'd been recovering from the birth. For a while, he didn't think she would ever forgive him for keeping the news from her until the doctor declared her strong enough to bear it.

"I'm sorry. Have I come on your regular day? I didn't mean to interrupt. I just—somehow I just ended up here."

She shook her head and closed the distance between them. "You're not interrupting. How would you even know I'd planned to come today? You've made a new friend."

"Chauncey. I'm thinking of making him a house dog. What do you think?"

She tilted her head, considering. "He looks well-behaved. I suppose we could give it a try."

As if aware he was under scrutiny, Chauncey perked his ears and sat straight up for a second—before taking off after a rabbit. "I'll work with him. He might need some training, or at least a little focus on his attention span."

"Will he be all right?"

Gabriel nodded. "He knows the grounds better than I do, maybe. He'll make his way back to the kennel or the house, at least."

"To be honest, I'm glad to see you. Many times, I've stood in this spot and longed for your company here. I think he would like to see us together." She gestured toward their son's grave.

"Do you think he sees us?" Gabriel slipped an arm around her shoulders.

"I don't know. Aunt Agatha says that he'll come back to us someday. I would like to believe it's true. In the meantime, perhaps he's all around us, keeping watch."

He liked that she was thinking of a future for them. All three of them. "I hope Father isn't filling his head with nonsense. 'Stand up straight. Be a man.'"

She laughed. "Goodness. He was only a baby."

"So was I at one time. It never stopped Father from saying such things." He rubbed a strand of her hair, fallen from her chignon, between two fingers. "Our son. He would be old enough to go to school."

"Not boarding school." She brought a hand to her chest in alarm. "I couldn't bear to send him away."

"At some point, he would grow up and be ready. We would have to let go."

She turned to face him, tears glimmering. "No letting go. Hold me, Gabriel."

"Of course." He pulled her against him, wrapping his arms around her.

She sobbed quietly against his shoulder while he patted her back, afraid to move and spoil the moment.

But she looked up. "I'm sorry. I always cry a little when I come here."

"It's only natural." He preferred it to her anger. The last time she was here with him, she wouldn't even look at him. "I miss him too."

"But after all these years? At some point, I should be able to face our loss with grace and dignity. Lord knows, I couldn't manage it when we—well, when I first heard that we'd lost him. That you'd already buried him. I was so distraught."

"You blamed me. I understood. I should have told you. I should have known that you could handle the worst. You're strong, Sophia. Stronger than I've ever acknowledged."

"I'm not strong. I'm determined. Throw a challenge my way and I'll accept. But expect me to survive another loss like the one we've had to endure, and I'm not sure I would make it."

He nodded. "I think we've had enough loss."

"But we don't get to decide. Fate does. God does. It isn't up to us."

"Then perhaps we should leave ourselves in the hands of fate and stop worrying so much that the worst will happen. As you say, it's not up to us. We can only live our lives expecting the best will come our way. We are good together, Sophia. Let me show you." He stroked her cheek and leaned in to kiss her.

"You're asking me?" She smiled, forcing him to pause. "Just like the first time. Remember? In the Duke of Enderleigh's garden? You asked if you could kiss me. I thought you were so delightfully old-fashioned and odd."

His eyebrow shot up. "You found me odd?"

He had imagined that he made an impression, but in his mind it was tender, strong, considerate. Odd?

"No one else had ever asked my permission before you came along."

"And a lot of men kissed you in the moonlight, did they?"

She shrugged. "A few. None of them as skilled as you. They kissed me, but quick pecks. You left me breathless. Only you."

"Because you gave me permission to do so. Do you see? Odd? Old-fashioned? No. I was a man who knew what he wanted. And once I had your consent, I didn't have to stop with a quick peck like the others, who were testing their limits. I knew you wanted me."

"I don't recall being that obvious." She smiled, her full lips curving until the bottom lip bowed up just a little in the middle. He'd never seen anyone else with a bottom lip quite like Sophia's, and he adored it. Her one imperfection, which of course only made him find her all the more perfect.

"All a man needs is a little encouragement, darling."

"I thought I was offering encouragement." Her tears were gone, but her eyes still sparkled as she looked up at him.

He wouldn't wait for another invitation. Dipping his head, he brought his mouth down and gently brushed his lips to hers. She tasted sweet, like berries, and tart. He couldn't fathom the tart. Lemonade? But he wanted more of her. His kiss became more insistent, until his tongue was tangling with hers and they seemed to share the same breath. She nipped at his lip when he started to back away, urging him to kiss her again and again, his hands smoothing over her curves.

"It's rhubarb," she said at last, breaking for air.

"I'm sorry?"

She laughed. "You looked like you were mulling something over. I might taste of rhubarb and strawberries. I stayed much longer than I expected at the farm. They had pie."

"I suppose I would have outstayed my welcome too for some of Mrs. Cooper's pie."

"I stayed to wait for Anna to gather her things. She's my new secretary." Her voice held a hint of triumph. Is that why she'd forgiven him? She'd found her secretary and she meant to show him up somehow?

"Anna Cooper? She's a child." What on earth did she expect to accomplish with Anna Cooper's assistance?

"She's sixteen. And a fast learner. She was so excited to be offered the position. Yes, she's young and will need instruction, but I knew I'd done the right thing by asking just as soon as I saw her face at the news. She's dreadfully bored at the farm, and a girl her age needs the excitement of new opportunities."

"She'll be living with us at the house then?" Every time he saw a way to reduce the number of guests and have more chance to be alone with his wife, a new one came along. Would he ever be rid of distractions?

Sophia nodded. "The room just down from mine, across the hall."

"Why not send her up to share with Mrs. Jenks? The two of them would get on fine. I'm sure Jenks could use a roommate."

"A secretary should command more respect than a lady's maid, don't you think?"

"Where has Mr. Grant been staying?"

"I thought it best that Mr. Kenner remain in the cottage for as long as he retained the title of estate agent," she said. "I assigned Mr. Grant to a room in the east wing."

"Near Lord Markham. But I suppose if Grant is to be my estate manager, I'll need to move Mr. Kenner out of the cottage and back into the house so that Grant can have the cottage…"

"Quite a muddle I've created." She didn't seem at all displeased with herself, despite the admission.

He laced his fingers with hers. "We'll work it all out in due time."

"Let me leave my flowers. I'll be a moment. Then we can head back to the house together."

Gabriel nodded, released her, and stepped back. Considering the circumstances, it was probably wrong of him to notice how her skirt clung to her curves, emphasizing her lovely bottom when she knelt at their son's grave. God help him, he was a man in need of the comforts that only his wife could provide.

The walk back gave Sophia a chance to cool down. Being alone with Gabriel made it too easy to forget that there had ever been any trouble between them. She felt carefree and spontaneous. But it wouldn't do to get caught up in the romance and forget the substance they lacked to make their marriage a true success.

"I didn't have the honor of seeing your mother this morning. I suppose she slept in." She stole a glance at him walking beside her, his athletic form apparent in his thin, white shirt. The day had grown warm, and he carried the coat he must have set out in when it was cooler.

He laughed. "I would hope so. She was in rare form last night. I have to apologize again for the surprise. I honestly had no idea she would arrive so soon."

"I wasn't expecting Lord Markham without notice either. Of course, I issued an invitation of sorts, but I thought he would send word when he meant to take me up on it. I hope I can count on your brother and Eve to take him in for a few days once they return to the countryside."

"Are they not at home now?"

She shook her head. "They're in London. I dined with them. They had just arrived on business and said they would be a few days enjoying some time without the children."

"Probably making a third." Gabriel laughed without mirth. "Some people take to it so easily."

"Eve had her share of struggles with her first husband. She supposed that it was her fault she hadn't conceived, but apparently she was mistaken."

"Apparently so." Gabriel kicked some brush out of their path and ushered her on, his hand remaining at the small of her back once they were well beyond the slight obstruction, a fallen branch. "I had no idea."

"You wouldn't. It's not polite conversation for the dinner table." She smiled. "I conceived fairly easily though, if you recall. We might be that lucky again."

"Are you ready to try? Does it appeal to you now, the idea of having children?"

She sighed. "The idea has always appealed to me, even if the reality still frightens me more than a little. I can imagine a time when I will be ready in the near future."

If things continue as they have, she wanted to add but did not. She couldn't chase the feeling that something could go wrong at any moment. She would say the wrong thing, or he would. One of them would give some hint that they had always been unsuited, and their world would unravel like the sweater she had tried to knit him the Christmas before he went away.

"It would be easier if we were on our own again like we used to be," he said.

"We've never been on our own. Not really. It's the burden of caring for such a large house and everyone we need to maintain it."

"Yes, but if we could be rid of Mother and Charles. Of the Waldens."

"And Mr. Grant? Ah, but you seem to have made your peace with him."

"I admire his business sense. It doesn't mean I have to like the man. I admire yours too. I probably should have said so earlier. It's just that I was preparing a surprise for you and I didn't want you to spoil it. There, I've said it."

"That's what you were up to this morning? It's not that you thought I was too...too feminine to be involved in business?"

"Not at all." He stopped walking and turned to face her, smoothing a loose tendril of her hair off to the side. "I knew you were angry with me. I tried not to upset you. Or rather, I tried to upset you just enough to chase you off, but I hoped not so much that you wouldn't speak to me again."

"Obviously, I'm still speaking with you. I felt much better once I got some air, a secretary of my own, and some pie. But don't think I'm that much of a pushover. I already have plans. I warn you that I'll not be nudged aside so easily."

"Duly noted, and as expected. Nothing is easy when it comes to you, darling."

"Why should it be? Now what is this surprise you have for me?" She narrowed her gaze.

"If I tell you, it will no longer be a surprise. I'm not ready to reveal it yet."

"I'm very curious by nature. That much hasn't changed. I'll find it out." She tilted her head and walked on.

He caught up in two strides. "And spoil your own surprise? You wouldn't. I know you too well. But just in case, I plan to keep you distracted."

"Distracted? How—" Before she could finish asking, he swept her into his arms and kissed her, not a mere brush of the lips. She opened her mouth, eager for him. Having him home again opened up a world of emotions, most of them good but some dangerous, like this overwhelming physical need. She couldn't recall ever having craved his touch so much in all of their years together as she had in the last two days.

His tongue, molten lava, slicked over hers, and she could no longer recall anything, not even her own name, until he moaned it low from the back of his throat. "Sophia."

Clearly, he'd gotten very good at distractions. She struggled to find reason through the fog that filled her brain, but all she could manage was a physical response. She reached for him, her hand skimming down his taut abdomen to pause at the top of his trousers.

His eyes glinted gold in the sunlight that spilled through the trees as he waited to see what she would do next. His hand covered hers when she paused, and he guided her attention upward to the buttons of his shirt, where he helped her undo the top few. She smoothed her hand over his bare chest, so tan and muscular. He'd spent some time without his shirt in Italy. She wanted to ask about it but found that the words were dry as ash in her mouth as she imagined him naked to his waist and lower. Her fingers splayed over his smooth skin, rediscovering him, the fine golden hairs bleached white from the sun, his copper nipples that pebbled at her touch, the ripples of his hard stomach.

He let her explore as he guided her deeper into the rim of trees, backing her against a bark-roughened trunk. "Is this what you want? Here? Now?"

A thrill coursed through her at the thought of him taking her against a tree, right out in the open. She felt a hot wetness at her core. Dear God, it had been so long, so very long. She still couldn't find her voice to speak, but she managed to nod.

"Not here. It wouldn't suit." His thumb stroked her lips. She rolled her tongue around the tip of it, eliciting his groan. "Or…"

"Please." She managed to get one hoarse word out. If not now, she might come to her senses and change her mind. She didn't want to change her mind, even if it meant spending the rest of her life in a mindless trance.

He cupped her face and took her mouth again, more fiercely, drinking her in like a man dying of thirst. She could feel him hard against her through her skirts. Desperate to feel him even closer, she parted her thighs and rocked her hips against him.

"Another minute and I won't be able to stop." His breath hot against her neck, he dipped his head to blaze a trail of kisses along her collarbone and lower. He'd expertly undone the top buttons of her dress while he was kissing her, as she discovered only after the fact when he slipped his hand inside her corset and tugged a swollen nipple between two fingers.

"I don't want to stop. Not now."

He took her hand. "Come with me."

She followed him to a gardening shed a short distance away. "Here?"

He opened the door and ushered her inside. "It's dark, quiet. There's an old chaise longue there in the corner."

She followed his gaze. Indeed there was. "I feel like a schoolgirl sneaking around."

"Exciting, isn't it?" He fluffed the cushion and a cloud of dust wafted up, catching the rays of sun streaming in broken fragments through the one small, dirty window. "We're not likely to be caught."

"A good thing. Can you imagine the talk?"

"I can't imagine anything right now but the

thought of you naked. Let's get you out of these clothes." He swooped her into his arms again, kissing her neck.

"You can loosen my stays, perhaps, but corsets don't come off easily." She laughed. "And it will take time to dress again properly. Let's just…"

"Your gown is light. It will be ruined." He unbuttoned her further and eased the dress down her shoulders. "Unless we remove it."

She was about to protest when he kissed her again as he worked at her buttons, and she gave up all thoughts of stopping him. As the cotton pooled around her legs, she stepped carefully out of the garment and allowed him to set it aside, draping it over a reasonably clean-looking crate. She stood before him in only her corset, chemise, and petticoat.

"Off with it. Everything. This is no time for modesty, Countess." His fingers unlaced her with deft precision, loosening her corset and removing it with surprising speed.

Reluctantly, she began to peel off the remaining garments as he abandoned his own clothes with such haste that she barely had time to get a good look as they were coming off. His broad shoulders and strong chest tapered to a trim waist and steely abdomen sectioned into six by well-defined muscles. His skin went from tan to white as he exposed his hips. And lower. Her breath caught. His erection stretched out from a thatch of golden curls. So many times, he had called her exquisite, but he was male perfection. A golden god. All hers.

Without another word, she reached out to stroke

him, relishing the feel of his rock hardness beneath his petal-soft skin. When she slid her hand up the length of him, around the tip glistening with a bead of wetness and down again, she wasn't sure if her knees would buckle first or his. He moaned from low in his throat as they fell to the frayed cushion together and his mouth found hers again.

Her need flamed into an inferno threatening to consume her whole. He stroked her cheek, her neck, her breast, taking his time, so tender. She couldn't control her response to him, wrapping her legs around him and urging his hips to meet hers, rolling her body into his and teasing the tip of his cock with her sex. "Please, darling."

He laughed wickedly, pulling away. "Only if you're certain."

"Gabriel." She reached for him, unwilling to be put off. She would do it all on her own if necessary. "Now."

He entered her, the devilish smile still in place as he met her gaze. "Better?"

She'd been prepared to answer until he slipped deeper inside her and she lost all power of speech. She tipped her head back and let her blissful sigh answer for her. At last, she felt complete, as if with Gabriel away from her, she had been scattered in pieces to the wind. And now, he was home, thrusting deep, kissing her, teasing her with his fingers all the while, creating a delirious tension in her every nerve that strained to bursting as she moved with him, desperate for him, calling out his name as she reached a fever pitch. He spilled himself inside her.

And she was whole again. At peace. At last. His body rested atop hers as their breathing slowed in rhythm, their hands clasped over their heads against the wood frame of the shed.

Ten

HE COULDN'T STOP KISSING HER. HER LIPS, HER NECK, her breasts, that little vein that pulsed along her collarbone. Buried deep inside her, the weight of the world falling off his shoulders at last, he kissed his wife and knew that there was no greater happiness than being inside her, reaching climax together.

Until he felt her pulsing around him, sighing as she buried her face against his shoulder, he hadn't been sure that she was enjoying it too. It all felt so rushed and clumsy, not at all what he'd planned in his mind. But it had been so very long for both of them. Next time, he would take his leisure, explore her properly, make her quiver beneath his touch. Next time, they would take hours in a proper bed, his or hers...

Theirs. His most ardent hope was that she would be ready to move back into a room they shared, a bed for two. He was about to ask her about the possibility when the door swung open and Brian Sturridge, the groundskeeper, entered.

"Lord Averford," Sturridge said, startled. "And the countess." He turned abruptly, his back to them.

"Forgive me. I had no idea. I heard noises, thought an animal had gotten in here."

Gabriel tensed but did not move a hair, aware that he had given his groundskeeper a good glimpse of his backside. There was nothing to be done for it. His body was the only thing shielding Sophia from exposure.

"What did you find, Mr. Sturridge? Rabbit? Raccoon?" A lad walked in after Sturridge and turned away as abruptly. "Oh! Uh. I'm going to go check on the roses."

"I'll come with you. Move along there, Jimmy." Sturridge shooed the lad out, shut the door, and ran after him.

As quickly as they were interrupted, they were left alone again. "I'm sorry, Sophia. I thought they were working in the orchards all day, far enough from here. I had no idea…"

Fortunately, her body wasn't shaking under his from anger. He realized that she was laughing uproariously.

"Oh dear," she said, once she caught her breath. "We'll be inspiring some bawdy conversations among the staff."

Playfully, she slapped his rear as he backed off her to reach for his clothes. "Do you really think they'll talk?"

"If it were only Sturridge, perhaps not. The man can be trusted." She nodded decisively. "But the boy? It's going to be all over the house, probably even the talk of the village. They're all aware of our estrangement, but that we've made love in secret? Out of the house on our own estate?"

"In the garden shed, for goodness' sake. How desperate can two lovers be?" He tugged his shirt over his shoulders. "You're right. News will travel fast and far."

"It's not so bad." She sat up on the longue and reached for his hand to steady herself as she got to her feet. "Maybe they'll stop thinking I'm a cold-hearted shrew, and you'll certainly be lauded as a hero. Rightfully so. If only they could know how much of one."

He wrapped an arm around her waist and dropped a kiss on her pale shoulder, his bare-naked goddess. She seemed in no rush to get back into her clothes. "Yes? I finished so quickly. I hoped you wouldn't think badly of me."

"Of you?" She arched a brow. "I'm the one who insisted, if I recall correctly. Something just came over me, and I couldn't stop."

"I'm glad. I didn't want to stop. I don't want to ever lose this intimacy between us again." He tipped her head up, a finger under her chin. "Do you understand?"

"I'm not sure it's as easy as it sounds. We still have obstacles."

"We'll surmount them. One at a time. First…"

"First, my clothes. I can't stand here all day bare as a—"

"Bare as a goddess? You can if I have any say in the matter." He soothed his hands down her arms and drew her close to him again.

"Oh no, my lord." She backed away and gestured to his growing erection. "Not again. Put that away.

It's dangerous. We can't stay in here all day, or they'll think we're at it again."

"I don't mind." He flashed her a grin.

She rolled her eyes but smiled back at him. "Get dressed, Gabriel."

"Let me help you first." He picked up her corset and held it backward, showing none of the skill he'd displayed in removing it.

Once they were both properly attired, they headed back to the house. Walking more slowly than they had earlier, Gabriel pointed out things that delighted him along the way. The garden overflowing with roses, though they kept some distance from it knowing that Sturridge and the garden boy were working there. A patch of mushrooms, the inedible kind. The low stone fence around the edge of the fields. The vibrant green of the grass.

"I missed that green in Italy. They have grass, of course, in patches, but not as green as ours and not stretching out as far as the eye can see."

"It's drier there, perhaps. Or the earth has more stone and clay," Sophia ventured.

"Do you know what I missed most?" She shook her head, not hazarding a guess. He went on. "Blue. I had the deep blue of the sea and the cerulean skies. But I couldn't find the blue of your eyes anywhere except in my mind. I dreamed about your eyes, darling. Every night."

She laughed. "I haven't been to Italy recently, but they do have cornflowers as I recall. Fields of them."

"They're as close as I could get, but not the same. There's a certain luminescence only found in your eyes."

"Says the world traveler. I'll have to take your word for it." She stopped walking, but not to hear more compliments on her eyes. "We're almost there. I hate to go in."

"But it's our home, darling." He took her hand. "Thornbrook Park. Where else would you rather be?"

"The garden shed had a certain appeal, didn't it?" She blushed. "If only we could have locked the door."

"I can't say it would have been very comfortable for any length of time, but at least we were alone. A rarity for us in the coming weeks perhaps, unless…"

"Unless?" She glanced up at him through her dark fringe of lashes.

"We could start sharing a room again?" he asked, hopeful. "It's one way to get more time to ourselves in an otherwise crowded house."

"Oh." She bit her lip. "I don't know, Gabriel. That's a big step. I'm not sure we're ready for that."

"Of course." He adjusted his cuffs, trying to appear detached even though he felt a keen stab of disappointment in her answer. "Wouldn't want to rush things along."

"I'm not ruling it out. I just need more time."

"I understand." He took her by the hand, a show of support though he didn't understand. Not at all. "Well. Shall we go in then?"

He led her up the stone walkway, took a deep breath, and pushed open the door.

❧

As soon as Sophia walked through the door, she knew everything had changed. She felt the shift as surely as if the floor had rocked beneath her feet. The magic that she'd found in Gabriel's arms outside the house had not followed them in through the door. Within these walls, they remained very much apart. How could it be? They both loved this house. Outside, they could lose themselves in the enchantment. Inside, they were all business, reality. And the reality was that she still wasn't entirely sure of him, or even of herself.

"There you are, Gabriel. I've been looking all over for you. Hello, Sophia." His mother paused at Sophia, looking her over top to toe. "What happened? You look a tad disheveled."

Dear God, it only just occurred to her that she must look a fright, having put herself together quickly and in low light. Basking in the afterglow, she really hadn't cared much what she looked like, an unusual departure for someone so concerned with appearances. Leave it to Gabriel's mother to call it to attention.

"It was quite a vigorous walk." She flashed a look at Gabriel but found that she did not blush. Soon word of their adventure would be out, but there was nothing wrong with a husband and wife having relations. The venue might have warranted some reconsideration, but so be it. She had no regrets. "I'll have to go put myself together properly."

"In a minute. First, come see what I've done. Or, you go on up, Sophia. Come along, Gabriel."

A ball of dread formed in her stomach, like something rank and curdled. What had Teresa done? She followed as Teresa took Gabriel's arm and led him into the drawing room.

"There. You see? It's all back as it should be, establishing a proper flow. Though I'll have to enlist some footmen to go through the attic and pull out the organza settee, my favorite piece." Pleased with herself, Teresa clasped her hands under her chin.

Sophia swept by her husband and his mother. Mrs. Hoyle stood off to the side while two of the footmen arranged an end table near the claw-footed green velvet sofa.

"Put it down. Don't touch another thing until further instruction from me." Disheveled as she was, Sophia managed to speak in her most imperious tones. "Mrs. Hoyle, I see we have much to discuss. I'll expect you in my office in one hour." An hour should give her enough time to put herself back together properly.

"Lady Averford thought you might like to see it again as it was, my lady."

Sophia, an artful and empty smile on her face, turned to her mother-in-law. "Teresa, I see you've had an entertaining morning. I know how you need to keep yourself amused. Thank you for this glimpse into Thornbrook Park's past. Perhaps you should take up a hobby. Some women your age like to quilt, I understand. Mrs. Hoyle can find you some fabric scraps from among your old clothes in the attic."

"Quilting? Me? I wouldn't know where to begin. I've never been skilled with a needle and thread. No, I'm much more suited to decorating and let me add that…"

"Good afternoon." Agatha, in a chartreuse-and-peacock ensemble, complete with a feather fan, came along at the perfect time, escorted by Lord Markham.

"We're just coming in from a walk. It's a lovely day. Have you been out too, Sophia?"

Bless Aunt Agatha. Sometimes Sophia wondered if she really did possess a sixth sense. She prayed that the same sense had kept Agatha and Lord Markham on the opposite side of the grounds, far away from the gardening shed. "Yes, Auntie. Gabriel and I have just returned."

"And someone's been playing with the furniture. Time for a change? I have to tell you that it's all wrong, dear. It had a certain flow, the way you had it. Now it's, forgive me, it's a jumbled mess."

Sophia smiled, genuinely this time. "It was just an experiment. It's all going back as it was."

"Thank goodness. Teresa, dear." Agatha turned from Sophia to Gabriel's mother. "I'm about to give Charles a reading. Tarot cards, are you familiar? Come along to the parlor, and I'll give you a spread too."

Teresa's cheeks burned as red as her tea gown. "Thank you, but I have plans to go up to the attic."

"Please reconsider," Lord Markham spoke up. "I'd hoped I could count on being entertained by two lovely women this afternoon. I've been so lonely."

"I suppose I could take some time." Teresa cast one last glance at her handiwork before agreeing. "You know I love to be in demand."

Sophia breathed a sigh of relief to see Teresa walking away. She turned to the footman. "Now, put it all back the way it was. Mrs. Hoyle, I believe you can direct them. And I'll see you shortly."

"One thing, Lady Averford." Mrs. Hoyle approached. "I'm not sure which office you mean."

"Not sure which office? The office I've been using for over a year now, of course. You know exactly the one." Mrs. Hoyle remained loyal to the Dowager Countess. Sophia would make it clear that Hoyle's continued employment relied upon her changing sides. There was only one woman at Gabriel's side in charge of Thornbrook Park, and it was not his mother.

"Lord Averford's office then?" She looked at Gabriel with a thin-lipped smile. Did the harridan mean to drive a wedge between them or at least to capitalize on their perceived separation? Sophia had always had a hard time getting on with Mrs. Hoyle, but she'd thought they had reached some understanding between them. Apparently she had thought wrong.

Gabriel stepped forward and draped an arm over Sophia's shoulders. "My office is the lady's office. The countess is more than welcome to conduct business affairs there as she has done so capably in my absence."

"Of course, Lord Averford. I didn't mean to imply otherwise. Let me get things settled here and I will join you in an hour, Lady Averford."

Sophia tipped her head in Mrs. Hoyle's direction. "That will be all for now. I'm going to freshen up."

"Allow me to escort you, darling. I seem to need a change of clothes too." Once they were out of earshot of the servants, he whispered, "Since we're both a little dirty…"

Standing one stair ahead of him, Sophia was nearly his height. She turned and splayed her hand on his chest. "Don't even think of it. We had our moment, and now it's back to business."

"Our moment? Ouch. I knew it was quick but…"

"Gabriel." She flashed him a warning glare and turned to continue up the stairs. "I need a bath."

"I can help you with that."

"Alone. You don't give up easily, I'll grant you that." She reached the top of the stairs. He grabbed her hand as he came up the last step.

"I'll never give up when it comes to you." He placed a kiss in the center of her palm. "I hope you'll allow me to join you when you reprimand Hoyle."

"I wouldn't call it a reprimand. More of a reminder, perhaps, to understand where her loyalties should lie."

"In that case, I believe we should make a united front. She needs to know that I stand behind you in whatever you decide to do."

"Thank you." She softened at once. Her knees might have quivered the slightest bit. "I appreciate your support."

"I'll see you in an hour." He turned on his heel to walk off toward his room. She'd expected him to put up more of an effort to seduce her again, but he'd apparently taken her word that she had no intention of a repeat performance. Even though the sight of him walking away made her sorry that she hadn't changed her mind in time.

❧

Gabriel admired the way Sophia took command of the situation with Mrs. Hoyle, effortlessly putting the housekeeper in her place. He'd taken a chair at the worktable in the far corner of the office, where he busied himself with a book while looking on. Sophia sat behind his desk as if she belonged there, and she probably did.

She had kept the place running smoothly for just under a year.

Sophia had changed out of her afternoon frock into a severe, gray silk blouse buttoned up all the way to the middle of her neck and paired with a figure-hugging skirt. The figure-hugging might have been a figment of his imagination. He hadn't actually gotten a good look at her skirt since she had been seated before he came in.

"I need you to understand, Mrs. Hoyle, that the Dowager Countess is a guest at Thornbrook Park. While I appreciate you going above and beyond the call of duty to make a guest feel at home, this does not include rearranging the furniture."

Hoyle nodded. "My apologies. I suppose I got carried away with nostalgia. I do miss the old days when the earl and his brother were boys."

The crafty woman had managed to both apologize and call attention to her senior position at the house at the same time. Not to mention that she was undoubtedly trying to provoke a similar wave of remembrance from Gabriel and hoping that he would interfere.

"Be that as it may, Mrs. Hoyle, I expect to be consulted before any changes in my house take place, cosmetic or otherwise." Sophia tapped a finger emphatically on the desk. "Considering the temporary nature of the furniture rearrangement, I'm letting this incident pass without formal reprimand. But keep in mind that I expect your loyalty at all times."

"I know, my lady. Again, I'm sorry for my lack of judgment this once. It won't happen again."

Sophia cocked a brow and got to her feet. "Very good, Mrs. Hoyle. I expect you're eager to get back to work. Don't let me keep you any longer."

"Do it again, Lady Averford," Gabriel said, once they were alone again. "That saucy arch of your brow."

She laughed. He would never tire of that sound. "I'm curious where Mr. Finch was in all this. I would have expected him to put a stop to the nonsense before it began. But then, I suppose he was also here during your mother's time."

"Finch is fiercely loyal to you," Gabriel said, reaching for her hand. "You can't imagine he didn't know about the Kenner and Grant situation the entire time, but he never said a word."

"You really think he knew?"

"I know he did. I could see the relief on his face when I figured it out. Not much goes on around here that Finch doesn't know about."

"Exactly my point." She let go of his hand to throw her arms up in confusion. "So why didn't he stop Mrs. Hoyle from rearranging my furniture?"

Gabriel shrugged. "It's not something he would want to get wrapped up in, is it? They're peers. I certainly wouldn't want to be on Hoyle's bad side and have to keep working closely with the woman."

"True enough. I suppose I should go and see how Anna's settling in."

"A moment more of your time, please."

"Yes, Gabriel? What is it?" She stepped closer. To his surprise, she looked almost like she hoped he was about to kiss her again. In fact, he had considered sweeping everything off his desk to take her then and there, but he couldn't be sure she would truly appreciate the gesture.

"This worktable." His mouth went dry. He could still make an attempt? No. "If we moved it out, we could fit in another desk. All yours. What do you say?"

"We could work in here together? Work together on running the estate?"

"That's the idea, yes."

"I'm not too…feminine for the job?"

He shook his head. "It's what makes you perfect for the job. You add a certain sensibility. But I can't promise that I won't occasionally make my way over to you and try this."

Testing the waters, he reached out and trailed a hand down her blouse, just over her breast and the stiff stays of her corset. She didn't back away. Instead, she boldly met his gaze. "I might like that. As long as we made sure to get our work done first."

"Business, then pleasure?" He nodded. "Yes, I think we can manage that."

Before he could take his chance on easing her to the desk, there was a knock on the door and their butler appeared.

"I'm sorry, my lord, for interrupting." Finch cleared his throat. "There's a man here from Higgins Farm. He's waiting in the drawing room."

"Higgins Farm?" Sophia pursed her lips. "I wonder what could be wrong. I'll meet him in the parlor. Send for Mr. Grant to join us please, Mr. Finch."

Without another word to Gabriel, she turned and rushed out after Finch. Had she forgotten he was there? He followed her. "We might not need Mr. Grant. I have him working on something."

"He'll want to be kept informed." She didn't even bother to turn around.

When they got to the drawing room, they found Anna Cooper engaged in conversation with the man from the farm. Gabriel would say he was more of a boy, a lanky lad all elbows and knees, little more than eighteen if even that.

"Anna, I see you're feeling more at home. You've met Ethan Nash from Higgins Farm?" Sophia could undoubtedly see that there was no need for introductions.

Anna nodded, never taking her eyes from the boy. "Yes. Ethan has come by Tilly Meadow once or twice. He's friends with Brandon."

Of course he would be, two lads of about the same age.

Ethan stood. "Good day, Lady Averford. I'm sorry to bother you."

"What seems to be the trouble, Ethan?"

Gabriel waited but was never introduced. He stood back and listened as the tall young man fingered the brim of his hat in his hands while trying to explain the problem to Sophia.

"Last week's rain caused the creek to flood, and now it's threatening our crops. It looked like it would level off, but it just keeps rising. It's as high as it was last spring," Ethan explained.

"After the winter snows." Sophia nodded. "I can't imagine the rain alone was enough to make it rise to that extent. I wonder if something happened downriver."

Ethan shrugged. "With Mr. Higgins away, I want to keep any flooding down but I don't have enough men. We've got to make sandbags and build them up at the water's edge. If you could spare a few to come help out? Garden boys, footmen?"

"With Higgins away? Where is he?" Sophia asked, more curious than demanding.

"His wife took the twins to visit her mother, and the boys fell ill. He went to help. They'll all be back in a few days, I imagine, but in the meantime…"

"He's left you in charge. Yes, that's quite a responsibility on your hands. Last time, Mr. Grant and I came to help. We can come along again. Oh, Mr. Grant. There you are. We have a little problem," Sophia called out to Grant standing in the corridor.

He entered the room and Sophia seemed all too willing to rely on him when she hadn't even cast a glance back at Gabriel. Back in her role of authority, she seemed to blossom as she explained the problem to her partner, the estate manager. How Gabriel longed to be the man she relied on in a crisis, but she hadn't given him a thought. Perhaps it's what he should expect after being out of her life for a year, but it came as a blow, especially after what they had just done. Forgotten so easily. Gabriel turned to go back to his study when Anna called him back.

"Lord Averford. I'm so happy to see you." Someone was. "Thank you for the position. I mean to do my very best. Mr. Kenner has already been working with me, thank goodness. I might be lost without him."

"Kenner is, is he? Good man. You could learn a

lot from Mr. Kenner." Gabriel had to wonder just a little at Kenner's motives. Anna was quite pretty, with a trim figure and long brown hair that reached her waist unbound, but she was so young. But then, Kenner seemed younger than his six-and-twenty years. Gabriel would have to keep watch on the situation, just in case. "And have you settled in?"

"Yes. It's so nice having a room of one's own. At Tilly Meadow, I shared a room with Emily."

"It's nice for now, but you might find that you get lonely. When you're used to having someone there, and suddenly she's not… Well." He looked at Sophia, still engaged in lively conversation with Mr. Grant and Ethan. "It can hit you unexpectedly. Fortunately, you're close enough to go back to Tilly Meadow and visit when you want. And of course, you can always invite Emily for a night or two here."

"That's exactly what the countess said. Emily would like that. But not right away. I mean to keep it all to myself for now."

"Good idea, at least until you become accustomed to your duties. My wife can be a strict taskmaster."

Anna's smile lit up her face, and possibly the entire room. She had her mother's angelic good looks. "Mrs. Dennehy warned me."

"Did she?" Gabriel laughed. "That's Mrs. Dennehy for you. She's an excellent judge of character. You'll find our Aunt Agatha to be equally forthright, if a little more eccentric."

"I met her. She complimented me on my aura, but I'm not sure what she meant by it."

"You'll find out soon enough."

"I expect that I will." Anna's attention was drawn to the farmer.

"You know each other well, then? You and young Ethan?"

"Not really well. I'm sorry. I don't mean to be distracted. There's flooding, apparently. I could lend a hand with the sandbags."

"You know about sandbags?"

Her brown eyes widened. "I have lived on a farm for some years now, Lord Averford. I've been called on to help with all kinds of work."

"Of course. Why not offer a hand? We can't stand over here being ignored much longer, can we? Let's go. Anna here has some expertise with stemming floods," Gabriel interrupted Grant before he could make another new and undoubtedly fascinating point. "We volunteer our services."

"We were just getting ready to go," Sophia said, looking from Gabriel to Grant as if being forced to choose between them. "It's hard work, Gabriel. Manual labor. Are you sure you're up for it?"

"I certainly couldn't stand idly by while my wife lends her services." It was certainly a new side to Sophia, this selfless volunteering for rough duty. Did she think him incapable or merely too highbrow to lend a hand? She had no problem volunteering her Mr. Grant for the work. "I can go instead of Grant. I've got Mr. Grant at work on something for me."

"Mr. Morris is researching the matter," Grant said. "My hands are tied until Morris gets back to me."

"Morris the solicitor?" Sophia's eyes narrowed. "Working on what?"

Gabriel ignored her. "You could be working with Kenner to draw up the papers in the meantime, Grant. I need you here. No point running off to the Higgins' place. Anna and I can go, and I'm sure we can round up some of the men from the yard."

"What if I have work for Anna to do?" Sophia crossed her arms. She would be stubborn, would she?

"Anna's just gotten settled. You haven't put her to work yet."

"I'm happy to take Anna." Ethan was bold enough to state his preference. "Anna, you can ride with me. What do you say?"

Anna brightened up. She took Ethan's arm. "Yes."

"I've only brought the pony trap," Ethan said. "There's room for two, but it's not quite what you're used to, Miss Cooper."

"Anna will ride with me," Sophia said authoritatively. "A young woman always takes a chaperone under such circumstances."

"I didn't realize the etiquette books included chapters on manners in the event of flooding." Gabriel smiled. "At any rate, I'll call Dale to bring around the car. I haven't been out to Higgins Farm since I've been home. It has been a year or two since Winthrop rebuilt the place." He leaned in to whisper in Sophia's ear, for her hearing alone. "Besides, I can't bear the idea of having you out of my sight for long. Not in that skirt."

Sophia tapped her foot under said skirt, which Gabriel could now see was indeed figure-hugging. He felt his anger dissipating in favor of yet another emotion, lust. Her cheeks reddened, but it seemed to be more from annoyance than interest. "If you insist. I suppose you must have a look to be sure that I haven't been neglecting our tenants. Why would you have any faith in me?"

There was no point in answering her when she'd chosen to take everything he said the wrong way. He went off to get his hat and arrange for the car, having no idea what he had done to upset her. As far as he was concerned, he'd been the neglected one. Perhaps he was simply reading her wrong. Where was Aunt Agatha when one needed her?

Eleven

GABRIEL PLANNED TO DIVORCE HER. IT WAS HER ONLY conclusion based on his suddenly cool behavior and his commentary with Mr. Grant. *I've got Mr. Grant working on something*, he'd said. Something that clearly involved the solicitor. And drawing up papers. Gabriel was pretending to be interested in her, in love with her, only to lull her into a false sense of security until he could spring his surprise on her: divorce papers.

His mother had probably planned the whole thing for him. "Here's how we can be rid of her once and for all." It explained Teresa showing up "unexpectedly." And Gabriel just happening to be at their son's grave for Sophia's monthly visit? He only had to ask the servants to know which day she typically showed her respects. What better way to work into her favor than by taking advantage of her maternal tenderness.

She slammed the hairbrush down so hard on her dressing table that Jenks came running from across the room where she'd been preparing Sophia's dress for the evening. Sophia would have thought that hours of hard work loading bags with sand and lugging them to the water's edge would have taken all the fight out of her, but no. Not that the men present had actually let her do much in the end. Now that she had a chance to think, she found her anger rising as swiftly as the waters of the creek and pond out at the Higgins' place.

"What is it, Lady Averford? Can I help?"

"My hand slipped." She smiled up at Jenks in the mirror. "All is well. I've had a change of mind on what to wear for dinner. Make it the new Worth."

"The cream silk with the black trim? I thought you were saving that one for a special occasion."

"My husband is home. Every night is a special occasion." Another chance to remind him of what he would be missing, should he leave her.

He had barely spoken a word to her at the farm, though they had worked side by side. His attention had been on Anna Cooper and on directing the garden boys they'd brought along. Despite bringing plenty of help, Gabriel had insisted on hauling the heaviest bags himself, as if he had something to prove to them all. Though she couldn't blame him entirely. She knew the feeling of having to prove herself. She'd done the same thing when she'd been called upon to help with the sandbags to hold back the springtime floods only months ago. Then, it had felt freeing to do the work, to show that she had the will to take on any challenge. If only Gabriel could realize the change in her and still love her for it.

"How romantic! I'll get it ready." Jenks's blush told Sophia that news had already spread around the house about the afternoon's adventure in the gardening shed. All of the servants were assuming that the earl and countess were rediscovering their love. Sophia had almost been fooled enough to think the same.

But was she imagining things? Gabriel had loved her so tenderly. And fiercely. And then tenderly again. It had been romantic, hadn't it? And lovely. And savage. It had been simply everything she dreamed their reunion should be, except not in a bedroom. But perhaps the unusual setting had made it all the more thrilling at the time. One way or another, she was wrong. Wrong that he really loved her, or wrong that he didn't care for her at all. Her only option was to use her head and hope her heart didn't lead her astray.

An hour later, she pasted on a serene smile, her finishing touch, and drifted down the stairs. Gabriel was there, pouring a scotch for himself and for Mr. Grant. Apparently, Grant had learned to not say no to Lord Averford. At the sight of her, Gabriel missed his glass and poured some scotch onto the table. Her smile became quite real.

"Good evening, gentlemen." She seemed to be the first of the women to join them in the drawing room. Finch approached with a cloth before Gabriel could bother with his own mess. He handed the crystal decanter to Finch to replace and came away with two glasses. Mr. Grant was too distracted to take his for a second, his mouth gaping slightly as he stared at Sophia.

"Good evening, Lady Averford," Grant stammered at last, taking his glass from Gabriel.

"Sophia." Gabriel gave a nod in her direction before heading to stand, back to her, at the window. He could feign nonchalance if he wished. She'd seen him spill his scotch. She knew she had achieved her desired effect. She looked breathtaking.

"Lord Averford says that you built up the shoreline spectacularly." Grant made conversation. "No chance of the waters rising to threaten the crops now."

"Yes. It was a simple matter. A lot of hard work, as you know, but we all managed. Anna knew exactly what to do. She should be down in a moment. I trust Ethan hasn't arrived yet." She imagined him, a simple country lad, back at the farm agonizing over what to wear for a dinner with fancy people. In the absence of the Higgins family, Sophia had felt it only right to extend an invitation to the young man. She wished she could tell him not to worry. They wouldn't make a fuss. Though she might have chosen to stick with a plainer gown to make the newcomers more comfortable. As usual, she'd only been thinking of herself.

"We've invited Ethan and Anna to join us for dinner. I felt it only fitting, considering that Anna is new here and Ethan seemed so grateful for her help."

"And Mr. Kenner will be joining us for a change?"

She nodded. "To get to know Anna better, since they will be working closely for the next few weeks until she has a better understanding of her position."

Gabriel turned around at that, his finger in the air as if he were about to say something. But perhaps he thought better of it and turned back around to the window.

What had come over him? It wasn't like her husband to be rude to guests, though Grant wasn't technically a guest. She had to suppose the cut to be intended for her. What could have upset him? She was the one who feared that he was planning to surprise her with a divorce.

"What is so fascinating out there?" She joined him at the window.

"Chauncey. The dog." He gestured with his glass and then downed the contents in one gulp. "He's chasing a squirrel, and I think he got him too. I'm surprised the kennel master hasn't rounded Chauncey up yet. I was thinking of bringing him in here."

"Not with that squirrel between his teeth you're not. I'm sure he's fine where he is for now."

"Perhaps for now."

"And he could probably use a good bath before he becomes a house dog."

The sound of footsteps caused them both to turn around to greet their guests. Aunt Agatha was colorful as always in fuchsia with canary-feather accents and a jeweled turban. She clung to the arm of Lord Markham, who had apparently helped her down the stairs. Was Agatha getting frail and Sophia hadn't noticed, or was she enjoying some male attention for a change? Sophia couldn't decide.

"Agatha." She stepped forward to embrace her aunt. "You're looking well."

There was a certain look of mischief playing in Agatha's cat-green eyes. What had she been up to?

"Thank you, dear. And you too. As usual. Charles and I keep bumping into each other."

"So you do. Good evening, Lord Markham." Sophia had decided that she was more comfortable on formal terms with Lord Markham, perhaps since Gabriel had seemed to take offense at her apparent intimacy with the man. Though perhaps she should rethink that. It wouldn't hurt to keep Gabriel on his toes.

"The Yorkshire air." He winked. "It has restored me. I thank you again for inviting me."

"It's our pleasure to have you. Isn't it, Gabriel?"

Gabriel hadn't gone back to the window, but he seemed out of sorts. "Scotch, Markham? I was about to get myself another."

"I don't mind if I do."

Sophia had never paid much attention to Gabriel's drinking. It had never seemed excessive or worrisome in the past. But now she wondered about it. Had he taken to drinking more in Italy? Drowning his sorrows? Or perhaps celebrating his freedom? Though she was so sore from the afternoon's labors that she nearly requested a glass of her own. Perhaps she shouldn't think much of it at all.

Mr. Finch had left his post by the cocktail cart, probably to stay near the front door since they were expecting more guests. He returned a minute later to announce the arrival of Ethan Nash. Sophia was taken aback to see the transformation in the man, from farm boy to what could have been a young gentleman. He wore a fine, dark suit, with his formerly unkempt hair tamed and brushed back from his face. He was much more handsome than she'd given him credit for, and she began to worry about Anna after all.

"Welcome, Ethan. Or should I call you 'Mr. Nash'?" She smiled in an attempt to put him at ease. "I'm so glad you could join us this evening."

"Thank you, Lady Averford. Ethan will do. I'm

happy to have the invitation. I can't stay very late. I'll need to get back to tend the livestock. But it's good to have the chance to feel civilized again."

Again? She wondered about his situation. Did he come from a good family? Merchants, perhaps? Or was he the son of a physician or lawyer? She hadn't expected him to have any experience with dressing for dinner, but clearly he knew their ways. He wasn't the bumpkin she'd expected him to be. So what had brought him to work on a farm?

"Ethan." Gabriel approached. "Good to see you could make it. Would you like a drink?"

"No, thank you, Lord Averford. Perhaps some wine with dinner. I was just telling the countess that I have to be in shape to get back early and look after the livestock."

"Ah, good lad. Responsibility above everything."

Anna made her entrance not long after Ethan's arrival, her simple pearl-gray gown flattering her despite its plainness. His whole face brightened up, but it was possibly from the relief of seeing an acquaintance closer to his own age. Anna had shown him some interest earlier, though not to any measure of great concern. But now? He looked entirely suitable, possibly even desirable for a sheltered young woman like Anna. Sophia knew she would have to keep watch over them. She hadn't coaxed a young girl away from her home and family only to expose her to the greater danger of falling in love too soon.

"Ethan, you came." Anna's freckled cheeks flushed with pleasure as she greeted the boy. "I wasn't sure you would make it. Oh look, Mr. Kenner has come down too. Let me introduce you to Mr. Kenner, Ethan. He has been such a help to me."

To Sophia's surprise, Gabriel came to stand by her, draping an arm around her waist. She felt a sensual thrill at his proximity. How could she want him so badly when she had so many doubts about him? She couldn't control her body's reaction to him, but she could certainly make sure nothing came of it again until she had made up her mind. Couldn't she? Glancing up to see that gold gleam in his soulful, brown eyes as he looked at her made her wonder.

"I don't like the way Kenner looks at her. We'll have to watch out for those two," Gabriel whispered for her ears alone.

"Kenner? I was worried about Ethan. There's more to him than I expected."

Gabriel sighed. "I suppose having a pretty, young girl in the house will be more challenging than we anticipated. Good practice. We could have a daughter one day. If she looks anything like you, we're in for a world of trouble."

"I do believe you've just paid me a compliment, Lord Averford. I thought we were on the outs."

"Why would you think so?" He kissed the top of her head. "Because I deigned to gaze out the window at a dog when you were in the room looking so resplendent? A man has to do something to hide his inflamed desire, darling. Especially when there are guests in the room. Were we alone, I might have already balanced you on top of the grand piano and…"

"Gabriel." She felt the heat of the blush rising to her cheeks. "Someone might hear you."

"So be it. If they have a problem with me wanting my own wife, well, to hang with them."

Agatha left Lord Markham and Mr. Grant in conversation and approached Gabriel and Sophia. "There's something different about you tonight, Sophia, a certain radiance that has been missing of late. I'm pleased to see the two of you together."

"We could probably attribute it to our afternoon walk, yes?" The wicked smile was in place when Gabriel looked at Sophia. "It was a vigorous walk. It did us both a world of good, I think. I was hoping we could do more walking in London. Tomorrow. I have some business and I want you to accompany me, Sophia."

"London." She nodded, considering. They could be alone again, but in London. She had determined that she would make a point of going with him more often, but so soon? She had just been there. "What am I to do there while you're off attending business? I suppose you imagine me staying at home, accepting social calls…"

They both knew no one would call on her. She had been away from that scene for too long, and good riddance. She didn't fit in with the London ladies. They would find her provincial or, worse, out of fashion.

"You've never objected to shopping. I would keep my business short to make sure we have plenty of time there together." Together alone. She knew what he wanted from London, and she didn't object. Perhaps it was time to expand her horizons.

"I'll think about it."

"I believe you should." Agatha winked at Gabriel. "London is the place for walking. Walking is good

for the body and soul. I do recommend more vigorous walks."

Agatha knew! Gossip had most assuredly already
made its way all over the house. Sophia shouldn't be
surprised. Of all the servants, Agatha's maid, Mary, was
perhaps the most unrepentant of busybodies. Too late,
Sophia recalled that she had also put Mary in charge of
dressing the Dowager Countess. As if on cue, Teresa
swanned into the room, wearing a nearly identical
gown to Sophia's.

"I'm sorry to have kept you all waiting." It was
just like Gabriel's mother to assume everyone waited
on her. In fact, they did, but it pained Sophia to pay
her any unnecessary attention. "Oh dear, I'm afraid
we're twins."

Fortunately, Teresa looked even more appalled at
the idea than Sophia felt. "I thought your new Worth
gowns weren't being sent for a few weeks."

Teresa sighed. "All but this one. This one I had to
have immediately. Jean-Philippe assured me it was one
of a kind."

Sophia cocked her head, looking it over. "It could
be. He's used the same fabric and same idea for both of
our gowns, but there are obvious differences."

Differences, besides that Teresa's fit like a shelf
designed specifically to put her ample breasts on display. Teresa's gown had black draping that crossed the
front in more of a Grecian style, while Sophia's pleated
under the beading on the bosom and draped to the
sides like a robe over her ivory gown.

"Still, I'll have words with Jean-Philippe. One of a
kind indeed."

"I wouldn't be too hard on him. We both have impeccable taste." Sophia tried to remain unflustered.

"You're stunning, both of you. This Worth fellow must be a genius to know exactly what becomes a woman most." Lord Markham smoothed over the faux pas of the two of them appearing in strikingly similar gowns.

"Shall we go in?" Gabriel took Sophia's arm.

She still didn't know what to make of him. How badly she wanted to put her heart in his hands and believe the best, but she couldn't afford to take chances. At stake was her whole way of life, her home, and her happiness.

❧

Gabriel couldn't imagine what was going on with Sophia. Was she angry with him or not? Did she regret their lovemaking or want more of it? If they shared a room, he would have more time with her to try to figure her out. The sooner he broke down her defenses, the better. To that end, he hoped she would say yes to accompanying him to London. He would take the opportunity to move along his plans to gift her with the land, which wouldn't take more than a visit to his solicitor's office, and they would have the rest of the time together. Perhaps he would slip into her room again tonight to try to convince her.

All through dinner, he tried to distract himself from his desperate urge to get her alone by keeping watch over the curious trio of Cornelius Kenner, Ethan Nash, and young Anna Cooper. Kenner seemed to have a passing interest in the girl, but nothing unseemly as far as Gabriel could detect. Working in proximity with her, Kenner might become more obvious with his intentions, if he had any.

Nash, on the other hand, seemed more at ease in a formal dining room than Anna Cooper did. More than once, Gabriel saw him silently gesture to indicate which fork she should use or how to cope with the footman's attentiveness at table. Gabriel suspected that Ethan belonged to one of the fine families in the area and had taken to farming as perhaps a sort of rebellion or out of a genuine interest in horticulture. He might be one of those fops who studied agricultural sciences at Oxford and then became interested enough to try to gain a better understanding of the principles in practice.

Anna Cooper, though, seemed to be exactly what Gabriel believed her to be, a sheltered young woman who hadn't a clue about the true motives of men. Gabriel would be concerned about Ethan revealing his undoubtedly privileged birth if Sophia hadn't already learned her lesson, twice, about the perils of matchmaking. Sophia could, in fact, expand Anna's social circle to include eligible young men she might not otherwise encounter, but in a few years perhaps. In the meantime, they both would take care to guard the young girl from unsavory situations.

Saving her tonight, perhaps, was that Cornelius Kenner had excused himself to get to bed early not long after dinner. Shortly after that, Ethan Nash had gone back to the farm. Gabriel wished he could get rid of the lot of them so easily, but Anna, Mr. Grant, Lord Markham, Aunt Agatha, and his mother remained for cordials in the drawing room. Mother insisted they play at charades. Gabriel hated charades, but he didn't want to be a poor host. The others, with the exception of Sophia who had remained aloof all evening, seemed eager to try a round.

Mother went first. She made a frame around her face and then dropped the frame. Every time she made the frame, she looked more and more sickly. Outside the frame, she always made the same exaggerated smiling face. Anna, overexcited, guessed at everything but never guessed right. Aunt Agatha barely suppressed a knowing smile and said she didn't dare guess and ruin the fun because she sensed all the right answers.

"*The Picture of Dorian Gray*," guessed Sophia, who hadn't seemed to be paying attention at all.

"Right!" Mother shouted, seemingly disappointed that Sophia was the one to figure it out. "Your turn."

"I'm going to need a little help." She nibbled her lip as if considering. Gabriel expected Sophia to choose Anna or Charles or even Mr. Grant out of the crowd, but she crossed the room to hold out her hand to him. "Please, do this with me. I know we both hate to be the center of attention."

He had to stifle a laugh, because the Sophia he knew loved nothing more than to be the center of attention. But he felt the need to take her seriously tonight. "All right. I'll follow your lead."

When she stood on tiptoe to whisper in his ear, her breasts brushed his arm. And when her hot breath streamed along his neck, he had to struggle for control of his body. He could never get enough of her.

"Just make that face," she said. "I'll do the rest."

"What face?"

"You know the one. You make it when you're trying to figure me out." She arched a brow and curled her lip a little in imitation.

He laughed. "I'm certain that I've never looked that way in my life."

"You've no idea." She laughed too. "Just do it. Come on."

She led him to the center of the room and positioned him in front of the fireplace.

"And so we begin," she said with a nod to the audience. She walked in front of him, back and forth, and looked back at him with a haughty expression, then pretended to whisper behind her hand to someone, studying him all the while. She shook her head in indignation and strode to the edge of the scene, presumably offstage, where she gestured it was the end of their Act One.

"I haven't a single idea." Mother was the first to speak up.

"I'm puzzled too," Markham agreed.

"*The Taming of the Shrew.*" Grant seemed to think he had it. For a minute, Gabriel was inclined to agree. But Sophia tugged his arm to whisper what they would do next.

"Dancing. Just pretend we're at a ball." She took his hands.

"I hate balls."

"Exactly. That will do." She nodded, satisfied, then took the lead and swept them around the floor.

They danced for barely a second before he insisted on taking the lead. She could make him act the buffoon if she wanted, but he would be damned if he'd be led around by his wife on a dance floor. He was the one to take charge, taking her more tightly into his arms and swaying with her to an imaginary tune. He swirled them left and right, and was tempted to dance her straight out of the room and kiss her breathless. Instead, he let go and bowed to her, his partner. She curtsied and scurried off to the side. He followed. The guesses began again.

"A ball of some sort?" Anna guessed.

"One of Alva Belmont's affairs, perhaps?" Mother offered. "Though not dull enough to be one of those."

Agatha clapped her hands as if delighted but never hazarded a guess.

Sophia shook her head. All wrong. And so it was on to Act Three. "Now, you get down on one knee as if you're going to propose."

"What the devil are we acting out?" He had no idea.

"You really don't know?"

"Should I?"

She waved him off. "Oh, probably not. Your brother might have guessed it by now. He's the bookish one."

Gabriel loved his brother. After years of sharing a contentious relationship, they were finally getting along. But still, comparing him to his brother was like waving a red flag in his face.

She went to the fireplace and pretended to be reading a book. He followed, dropped to one knee, and pretended to propose, holding out his hand to her. She smiled and looked delighted, as expected, then suddenly she narrowed her gaze, shook her head vehemently, and pointed him to the door.

What? She was saying no? To him? And after such a perfect pretend proposal? The nerve of her! He got to his feet, ran a hand through his hair, and turned on his heel to leave.

"Oh!" Anna cried out. "I know it! I do. I really do this time!"

"Well, young lady, that beats the rest of us." Markham laughed. "What is it?"

Anna got up. "Obviously, he is all pride. Well done, Lord Averford. And seeing his pride, and his wounded pride, and that look on Lady Averford's face…"

"What look?" Gabriel asked. She had a look too, did she? He hoped it was every bit as ridiculous as the look she had accused him of having. But no.

"This." Anna mimed Sophia's face, and it was beautiful, naturally. His wife was incapable of looking anything other than beautiful, no matter what she did. "Why, it's prejudice, of course. They've acted out *Pride and Prejudice*. It's my very favorite book in all the world. Tell me I'm right!"

Sophia applauded. "Yes, Anna. You've guessed correctly."

"*Pride and Prejudice*?" Gabriel asked, confused. "And I was acting out pride? Why didn't you say so? It might have made my job easier."

"Oh, darling." Sophia laughed. "You're the very picture of pride at every moment. How could you go wrong? But you were not actually personifying pride. You were my Mr. Darcy."

"Who?"

"Darcy. He's a character that girls adore," Anna said consolingly. "I'm sure you haven't read any of it."

"No, I don't think I have." Gabriel shook his head. "But this Darcy fellow had better be a catch."

"Oh, he is." Anna hugged her clasped hands to her chest. "It's a very good book."

Teresa rolled her eyes. "It's mediocre. I prefer *Jane Eyre*."

"You would." Sophia laughed. "You probably wish Gabriel had a first wife in the attic to scare me off."

"Sometimes I do." Teresa smiled. "Have you checked recently?"

"The only things in the attic are all of the old things that I've replaced with new." Sophia had been joking at first, he'd been certain. But suddenly her words held an acerbic tone.

Teresa raised a brow. "You can't find true quality these days. Not like we used to have. Some of those things in the attic are treasures. Timeless treasures."

"My, it grows late." Gabriel felt it time to step in. He didn't like where the conversation was headed. "Perhaps it's time that we all went up to bed."

Fortunately, Gabriel's suggestion was met with approval all around.

Twelve

Sophia felt the tension growing in her veins, ratcheting up until she might have done something foolish, like irreparably damage her tenuous relationship with Gabriel's mother. She was glad when Gabriel suggested they end their evening, even if it meant that he would probably insist on escorting her so he could attempt another seduction.

"Gabriel, a moment." She took his arm as they headed toward the stairs after making sure all of their guests had gone up. "I have such a headache."

"Let's get you to your room and we'll ring for Jenks."

"No. She'll only have to come back down, and why give her the trouble? We can simply go back to the drawing room and have Finch bring me a glass of water. I think that's all I need. Some water. I might have had too much wine at dinner." She hadn't. She'd been keenly aware of staying on her guard.

What she did have was a case of suspicion. Jealousy, if she were being honest. She had seen the way Gabriel couldn't take his eyes off young Anna at dinner, and it concerned her. Bringing Anna into the house might have been a mistake. She was young, granted. Perhaps a little too young to tempt a man of Gabriel's stature. But she was a pretty girl with an admirable figure. High, firm breasts and narrow waist.

She was old enough for a dalliance, if it came to that. Cornelius Kenner and Ethan Nash had both seemed a tad smitten with her, and who could blame them? Anna's brown hair had been pinned up at dinner, but both Gabriel and Sophia had seen the girl running around the farm with her brothers and sister, her hair flowing down to her slender backside.

"Finch." Gabriel saw the man in the hall and gestured him over. "Please fetch Lady Averford a glass of water. Do we have anything to ease a headache?"

Sophia held up a hand. "No, just water is fine. Thank you, Mr. Finch."

"Right away, my lady."

Gabriel escorted Sophia to the settee, insisting she have a seat while they waited. "And let me guess, this headache started right around the time Mother showed up in a dress entirely too much like your own?"

She shrugged. "Not at all. I arrived first, and I had already made my desired impression by the time your mother arrived. If anything, I found it all rather amusing."

"You certainly stole her thunder." Gabriel adjusted his cuffs, probably eager to undress.

Inadvertently, her mind flashed to the image of him stark naked in the gardening shed. Admittedly, he had an impressive physique, but she couldn't allow herself to get caught up in physical attraction. She'd had her afternoon. Why hadn't once been enough?

"I like to think so. She looked crestfallen to see me in a similar gown." Sophia smiled. "Do you think she's interested in Lord Markham?"

"Lord Markham?" Gabriel shook his head. "I might expect her to sink her talons into Mr. Grant. She likes younger men."

"A woman can change."

"I've no doubt." He met her gaze. "To be honest, I haven't paid much attention to Mother. I'm more concerned with Anna Cooper."

"Anna Cooper?" Sophia felt her mouth go dry as ash. Did it run in the family, a preference for younger prey? "Why have you been intrigued by her?"

He laughed. "I didn't say I was intrigued. You make me sound like a lecher. I'm merely concerned for her welfare, a young girl that we've taken into our home. I feel somewhat responsible for her. Don't you? I thought we agreed on this."

She shook her head as if to clear all unsavory suspicions. "Of course we did. You're right. I have concerns as well. Both Ethan and Mr. Kenner seemed to have shown her some interest."

"Exactly." Gabriel nodded. "Ethan couldn't take his eyes off her at the field. She has a womanly figure, but her face is so young. She's out of her depth. I hope that Kenner and Ethan remember that they're dealing with a sixteen-year-old. And not a very mature one at that."

"I wouldn't say that Anna is immature. She has been helping on the farm and with the care of her younger siblings for many years now."

"But she's an innocent, not attuned to the ways of the world."

"Uncertain of men, perhaps. But so many of us are, no matter what our range of experience. For example, I'm not sure I'll ever figure you out, Gabriel."

"Ah, so we've come to it. The true source of your headache is trying to solve the puzzle of your enigmatic husband. And I thought I was so transparent." He placed a hand under her chin and tipped her face up to meet his. "You know what I want."

"I think we've both established what we want as far as a physical connection. That's not what troubles me."

"Count yourself lucky. It plagues me to no end wondering when I can get you in my arms again. It's nearly all I think of, day in and day out."

She tilted her head. "You're a man. It's to be expected. I think deeper thoughts."

"And that, madame, could be at the heart of your problems. Satisfy the simple urges first, and you might find that the answers to the deeper issues just present themselves along the way."

"My urges don't feel all that simple."

"Oh? When you know what you want, it couldn't be simpler. Man, woman, the way we fit together. Watching you exert yourself at the farm, the color in your cheeks, it made me want you all the more. I've never seen you that way."

"Lifting heavy things? Trying to be useful to others? No, I imagine not. Most women try to avoid exerting themselves, at least in front of witnesses."

"They're fools then. You've never been more enticing."

A maid returned with Sophia's water, bringing an end to their repartee. "Water, my lady. And Mrs.

Mallows insisted on brewing ye a cup of her magic elixir. She says it will cure all that ails you, and then some."

"Where's Mr. Finch, Jane? And what are you and Mrs. Mallows doing up at this hour? Shouldn't you all have gone to bed hours ago?"

"Mr. Finch is helping Mrs. Mallows. She's up starting a broth for tomorrow's aspic. She said it needs time to simmer and develop the flavor. She won't be much longer. As for me, I'm afraid I'm not much of a sleeper. I like to be useful as long as others are up and working."

"That's commendable, but I do hope you'll get some rest soon. Mrs. Hoyle expects all maids up bright and early, as I'm aware, and she won't take staying up late to be helpful as an excuse." Sophia shuddered. "Why aspic? Mrs. Mallows knows I don't care for it."

"The Dowager Countess has a taste for aspic. Mrs. Mallows thought she would appreciate an extra course."

"Very thoughtful of her, but as unnecessary as the elixir. Since she went to the trouble though, I might as well give it a try. Thank you, Jane. You can run along to bed. Don't let us keep you."

Jane smiled sweetly. "Thank ye, my lady. Lord Averford. Good night."

Sophia took a hesitant sip. "Oh, it tastes terrible."

"That's why you should drink it all in one gulp. Mrs. Mallows knows her elixirs. Bottoms up," Gabriel encouraged.

Sophia wrinkled her nose. Easy to say when he didn't have to drink it. But she did as instructed, tipping the cup back and swallowing the vile mix in one gulp. She shuddered. "Ugh, it burns."

"Burns?" He took the cup and sniffed it. "Ah, I do believe she's brewed a potent cup. I detect a whiff of whiskey, among other things. Drink the water. It will help wash it down."

"Whiskey? Oh my. Well, I guess we now have some idea how Mrs. Mallows cures all ills. More power to her." She drank the water, every last drop. "It does ease the burn a bit."

"Feeling any better?"

She rubbed her temples. "I suppose I do. My head feels clearer."

"To bed then?" He offered her his hand.

She looked up at him. "I'll let you walk me up."

He nodded. "Understood. Come along."

She got to her feet and felt her knees give way under her. "I seem to be a bit wobbly."

"Wobbly?" He caught her before she went down. "Indeed. Wobbly. So it seems."

"Am I—could I be a little drunk, Gabriel?" Visions of swirly patterns danced before her eyes. She grabbed on to him for dear life, or at least to keep her balance.

"I guess you could be. The whiskey on top of wine for dinner, and what all else she put in there. Though, it has come over you quickly."

"What all else?" Her clear head suddenly became invaded by a wave of fog. Pea-soup fog. She could see, but she couldn't easily form a rational thought. She tried to take a step and ended up collapsing against her husband. And laughing! She started laughing and she couldn't stop. "I can't seem to walk."

"I'm sorry? Darling, you're not speaking clearly."

In her mind, she was. "I said take me to bed, my golden god of a husband."

"I heard that well enough." He lifted her in his arms. "You're drunk, all right. Hang on. You don't weigh all that much, but enough that I'm not sure I can make it up the stairs. Arms around my neck."

"Yes, my lord." She followed his instructions as far as she could tell. She might have actually grabbed on to his lapel instead of getting her hands around his neck. "Anything you say."

"Anything? I'll have to ask Mrs. Mallows to brew more of this elixir if it makes you so agreeable."

A prick of anger burned through her haze. "Are you saying I'm not agreeable? I'm always agreeable."

In answer, he only laughed. "Perhaps it's for the best that you try not to talk. You're only speaking nonsense."

She fumed silently in his arms, jostling with every step as he climbed the stairs. Seconds later—or was it minutes?—she felt her anger fade into the fog, replaced by another equally hot sensation. Lust. She burned for him. Every nerve, every fiber. "Gabriel."

"Yes, darling, we're almost there." A minute later, he placed her gently on her bed.

"Don't leave me." She tugged him back by the lapels.

"You're asking me to stay? All night?"

She nodded. "Please."

He sat on the bed beside her. "Then how could I possibly refuse?"

❧

Gabriel would spend the night in Sophia's bed. How he'd dreamed of spending an entire night at his wife's side! But he wouldn't lay a hand on her. Not in her compromised state. What had Mrs. Mallows put in the elixir? He doubted it was merely alcohol, though Sophia's symptoms did seem a lot like an advanced state of intoxication.

But despite her assertion that she'd had too much wine at dinner, he had barely seen her take more than a sip or two, and he had watched her fairly steadily throughout the meal. She'd passed on cordials. Then suddenly, the elixir and *wham*! Barely coherent speech and an inability to stand on her own two feet.

He would have to ask the cook about it tomorrow. For tonight, his chief concern was getting Sophia safely settled in bed. Would she be sick? Feeling terrible in the morning? He had no idea what to expect, but he planned on being at her side in any event. He wondered if he should call her maid or undress her himself. Did Jenks come to her at night without being called? He had no idea.

"Sophia?" Her eyes were closed but he couldn't be certain if she had fallen asleep. "Darling?"

"Gabriel." A slow smile spread over her lips, and then her eyes shot open. "Why aren't you beside me? Are you trying to sneak away?"

"Absolutely not. I was wondering if I should call your maid to help you undress."

"You could help me."

"I'm afraid you might not feel the same in the morning. I'm calling Jenks."

"You don't want to undress me?" She rose, pouting, and sat on her knees.

"I'll not take advantage of you in your current condition. I'm not sure what you'll remember or approve of come the dawn. If you haven't noticed, you're somewhat impaired."

She nodded. "There's a fog in my brain."

"Should I get you some coffee?"

"Blech." She made a face. "Only if you want my stomach to turn. No coffee. But I am sleepy."

"Then you should sleep. Sleep might be all you need." Before he could finish his sentence, she was sleeping. Soundly. Snoring a little, in fact, but it was an adorable little attempt at a snore, if anything. The kind of snore that would only come from a newborn kitten or his exquisite wife. "That's it. I'm ringing for Jenks."

The last thing he needed would be for Sophia to wake up, suddenly sober, and demand to know why he was undressing her. Jenks appeared not a moment after he rang.

"Mrs. Jenks. I'm sorry to bother you." Jenks was still dressed in her habitual black, her hair smoothed back in a perfect bun. Did she stay that way every night, completely dressed and presentable, just waiting for Sophia's final call? She probably did, he realized. It was her duty, after all, and she was paid well for her service. Better than all of the other maids anyway. Plus, she had the pick of Sophia's cast-off gowns, which were usually only worn once or twice. Not that Mrs. Jenks had much occasion to wear them… "Jenks, we have a situation."

"I can see that, my lord. Too much drink?" She peeked around him to glimpse Sophia asleep in bed.

Gabriel shook his head. "I don't think so. She had a headache and Mrs. Mallows gave her an elixir."

"Dear God, not Mrs. Mallows's magic elixir again."

"Again? You've heard of it?"

Jenks nodded. "Do you remember last year when the head housemaid, Nan, was sick for a week? Oh, sorry. You wouldn't. You weren't here."

"Sick for a whole week? From the elixir?"

Mrs. Jenks placed a hand to her apron. "Goodness, no. Mrs. Mallows convinced her to take the elixir as a cure. It worked, but she slept for a day and a half solid after taking it."

"A day and a half? What's in it?"

"Chinese herbs. That's all Mrs. Mallows will say. I think it's all she knows. She says it will cure all that ails you—"

"And then some." Gabriel nodded. "And she's still making it? Where does she get these herbs?"

"Her son is in China."

"Gilbert Mallows went to China?"

"He's exploring Eastern medicine. And who knows what all else. He's in love with a woman over there, says Mrs. Mallows. She doubts he'll ever come back home. But he sends her things."

"Like the herbs?"

"And a silk kimono. It's beautiful. Oh, and some funny bamboo shoes with velvet straps that go between the toes. Anyway, I wouldn't count on the countess waking up any time soon. But she should feel right as rain when she does."

"She doesn't like the rain." Concerned, he glanced back at his wife.